Choices They Made

Ashok Shenolikar

ISBN 10:1984196561
ISBN 13: **978-1984196569**
Library of Congress Control Number:**2018901669**

Your life is determined by the sum of

choices that you make.

—Frank Sonnenberg

Acknowledgments

If it wasn't for my son Sachin's suggestion a few years ago that I attempt writing fiction, this story would not have been written. Prior to this I was writing mostly nonfiction. This book started as a short story and then gradually developed into a series of connected stories.

My colleagues at the Northern Virginia Writers' Guild read all the earlier versions of the stories and offered terrific comments to improve the storytelling.

Kathryn Johnson of www.writebyyou.com was my writing coach and developmental editor. She helped me through the reorganizing and replotting of the story for it to be stronger. Thank you, Kathryn.

My daughter Sukanya and my dear friend Shekhar Tipnis diligently reviewed the proof of the book and made constructive recommendations to enhance the quality.

Lastly, my wife, Bharati, was always there to brainstorm preliminary ideas before I put them in the book.

Cover design by Emily Yahn.

Preface

Choices They Made is a collection of connected stories that follows four people across two continents as they try to fulfill their dreams. When they enter middle age, their paths cross again after 30 years, causing their lives to take an unexpected turn.

Ashok Shenolikar

Part 1
Ashley
1963

Ashok Shenolikar

Chapter 1

The letter from the landlord said that the room I had rented would not be ready for at least a month or more because the house had to undergo major plumbing and electrical repair. They addressed me as "Miss," as frequently happens. Because my name is Ashley, they assume I am a girl. The fact is that my mom was reading *Gone with the Wind* when she was expecting me, and she loved the Ashley character so much that she decided to name me after him.

The spring semester at the University of Oklahoma, Norman, was to start in a week. With the unexpected unavailability of the room, I was at a loss as to what to do and where to stay. Being a graduate student meant I had to stay off-campus. *Not a big deal*, I thought. I was sure the dean of students would help me out. Dad had said that he couldn't support me financially on his meager savings. The savings I had from summer jobs, mowing lawns, was sufficient to stay in a hotel for a day or so, but I had to act fast to get something permanent.

I took a Continental Trailways bus to Norman. It was the cheapest deal to travel from Phoenix. I booked a room at the Holiday Inn. It was early January 1963. As I combed my hair the next day in preparation to go the campus, I wondered what the meeting with the dean was going to be like. His phone had been busy every time I called from Phoenix, and I couldn't get on his calendar.

It had snowed. The roads on the campus were covered with a white blanket. As I climbed the steps to the dean's office, I slipped and tumbled down two steps. It was around nine thirty on a Friday morning, and the campus was almost empty. I tried to get up but slipped again. Somehow I managed to get up on my hands and knees and started climbing the steps. A young girl came from nowhere and asked if I needed help.

"No. I'm fine. Thanks," I said.

"Okay, but just be careful at this time of the year." She disappeared just as suddenly as she had appeared. She looked slim and attractive, even with her winter jacket and ski cap. I would have liked to talk to her more.

No way to start the day at a new place. What's the dean going to think of me with my hair disheveled and snow all over my jacket? I brushed the snow off my clothes; my fingers combed my hair back as I approached the dean's office. *Will the dean see me without an appointment?*

It was not going to be. The dean's secretary informed me that he would be out of town for a week and he would see me then, if I made an appointment.

My heart throbbed as I left the dean's office, and I felt hot in spite of the cool weather outside. I suddenly felt alone. Mom was right. I didn't know anyone in this university town, and what if the dean couldn't help me next week? What was I going to do for the whole week ahead? The meager money I had was to be used for books and food, not for a hotel. I didn't want to think anymore.

I crossed the campus and came upon a busy street, watching every step as I walked lest I slip and fall again. There was a small building with a red neon sign flashing the word "Rickner's" on the other side of the street. It looked like a diner, but it turned out to be a bookstore with a coffee shop in it. This was a good place to have a sandwich and coffee or a light snack. When the light turned green, I crossed the street, my nose and ears turning numb from the cold.

The store wasn't crowded. A young couple was browsing the books aisle, not talking much. I walked up to the counter and started to read the menu. I was in no rush. A young, freckle-faced, red-haired waitress was cleaning the counter with a white cloth in a circular motion. She looked at me and smiled but didn't say anything.

"Well, well. Isn't someone waiting patiently for a cup of coffee?" I heard a voice behind me. For a moment I thought I was obstructing someone wanting to proceed along the line. But there was no line. I turned and noticed a student, slightly shorter than me, wearing blue wranglers, a heavy winter jacket, and a maroon baseball cap with the letters *OU* on the front.

"Hi, I'm Owen. New here?" he asked, extending his right hand. I shook his hand as I wondered how he knew I was new in town. Perhaps I looked lost.

"Ashley," I said. "Ashley Wilkins."

"Isn't that a girl's name?"

"I'm asked that a lot. It's my mom's favorite. She named me after the character in *Gone with the Wind*."

"You from around here?"

"No. I came from Phoenix, yesterday. And you?"

"Pauls Valley. Not that far from here."

"How far?"

"Oh, maybe an hour to an hour-and-half drive."

"How come you chose OU?"

"Parents. My mom and dad thought OU is as good a college as any in the country, and they wanted me to be close."

Aren't all parents alike?

The red-haired waitress had finished cleaning the counter and was facing us, tapping her fingers on the counter, waiting for us to order something. I wasn't that hungry.

"A grilled cheese, please," I said.

"American, Swiss, or provolone?"

"American."

"Rye or white?"

"Rye."

"You want fries with it?"

"Uh, yes, okay."

God, I just want a sandwich, girl. I didn't know there were so many decisions to make. I had the American on Rye with fries. Owen ordered just coffee. We found an empty table and continued our conversation.

"So, where are you staying, Ash? Can I call you Ash?"

"I don't have any idea where I am staying, to tell you the truth. I went to see the dean this morning, but he is away. Returning next Friday. I had hoped he could put me somewhere. I am stuck at the Holiday Inn until then. I really don't think I can afford to do that."

"Weren't you assigned a dorm before you came here?"

"No. I'm a grad student. I have to stay off-campus."

"You could have rented a room before you came here."

"I had, but it was a last-minute cancellation. The landlord has to do some heavy repairs."

"Oh, crap. What're you going to do now?"

"No idea."

"Hey, I have an idea," Owen said. "My roommate Cody is

joining school a week late. You can stay with me until then."

"No, no. Are you sure? You don't even know me. What if I'm a criminal hiding from the police?"

"You don't look like one. Besides, my dad says trust God and he will take care of everything."

"Really?"

"Yes. He should know. He's a pastor in Pauls Valley."

"How much will I owe you? I'll pay you back when I start getting my stipend."

"No need. The room's been paid for."

I wasn't sure if it was legal for me to stay in the dorm, but I was willing to take the chance.

Owen's gray four-door Renault Dauphine was parked outside Rickner's. We drove to the Holiday Inn to pick up my belongings. Owen stopped by the checkout counter and talked to the clerk. I didn't ask him what it was about.

Owen's room in the dorm was standard university stock: two beds along the walls facing each other, tables with portable lamps, and small bookcases for each student. An OU banner and a calendar showing sports events hung on Owen's side of the wall. He even had an OU coffee mug on his desk.

After we dumped my stuff in Owen's room, he took me for a ride around town. It was three o'clock when we came back to his room.

The phone was ringing as we walked in. Owen answered. He talked for about five minutes. I heard him mention my name, so I guessed he was talking with Cody. At one point he squinted his eyes as if to concentrate.

"Shit," he said, after he hung up, almost slamming the phone in the base.

"What's up? Is everything okay? Was that Cody?"

"Yes. He's changed his plans. He's coming back next Tuesday. Three days from today." He looked worried.

"That's okay. I can move back to the hotel, if it comes to that."

"No. I get pissed off when people change their plans."

"That's okay," I said, but I was a bit worried too. It meant I had to get out in two days and then was at the mercy of the dean and then who knows what. Maybe there was a church that would allow me to stay free for a few days.

Chapter 2

Owen left me in his room and said he was going to run an errand. He slammed the door as he left. I collapsed on Cody's bed. When I woke up, it was dark outside. Owen hadn't returned. I turned on the radio, which was set to a country music station. I wasn't much of a fan of that kind of music but I didn't want to do anything to disturb my host. A few minutes later, the weatherman reported that there was a chance of snow flurries at night but the next day would be sunny. After an hour or so, Owen showed up. He looked more composed and calm.

"You hungry?" he asked.

"Yes. What do you have in mind?"

"Pizza?"

"Fine with me."

"The Pizza Hut on Lindsay is running a special. A dollar nineteen for all-you-can-eat pizza with iced tea," he said.

"Sounds like a good deal," I said.

While we were having dinner at Pizza Hut, Owen mentioned that he had planned to visit his folks in Pauls Valley the next day, to attend his younger sister Dana's sweet-sixteen birthday party.

"You're welcome to come with me, unless you have something to do here."

"Thanks. But I'd rather not."

"No?"

"I think I should spend time looking for a room."

"How're you going to do that? Walking around town?"

"That would be one way."

"Are you crazy? You'll freeze your socks off walking in this weather. Besides you don't know the town."

"I know."

"Look. Come with me, and I'll take you in my car to search for a room when we return."

As we were returning to the dorm, a few flurries started to fall. The weatherman was right. On the way back, we stopped at the Dairy Queen and picked up hot chocolate.

The phone was ringing again as we entered his room. Owen picked it up, said just a minute, and handed it to me.

"It's for you."

"For me? Who would be calling me here?" I wondered if the dean had returned early. I realized there was no chance of that. How would he know where I was?

"Hello," I said.

"Ashley, my baby!" It was Mom. "Where've you been? We have been trying to call you and see how's everything."

"I'm not a baby, Mom. I told you not to call me that."

"You are to me and always will be."

"How you got this number?"

"Well, we called the hotel where you said you were going to stay. First they said that you had left. We really got worried to hear that. Then the person said to wait and gave this number. Are you all settled? Who're you staying with? Is he a nice person?"

"Slow down, Mom. I'm okay. Don't worry. I met Owen this morning, and he has been extremely helpful."

"Who's Owen?"

"That's the guy I'm staying with."

I didn't tell her that this was a temporary situation.

"Well, thank him from us."

"I will."

"Okay, then. Don't forget to call us every day, and you take care."

I put the receiver down and turned to Owen. Fortunately he was busy looking through a magazine. I hoped he hadn't heard everything, especially the baby part. He looked at me and didn't say anything.

Owen didn't have a TV. We sat across from each other—Owen on his bed strumming his guitar and me on Cody's bed. It was easy to talk with Owen about the Vietnam War, student's drinking age, and our religious beliefs. It was obvious that he came from a religious family.

At one o'clock, we called it a night.

I slept well but had a dream. In the dream I walked into the dean's office, and he said he couldn't help me. According to him, the best way was to just go around the town and look for a vacancy sign. I had no car, so I walked and walked without finding any signs for rooms to rent or for roommates. I was tired and hungry and wanted to go home. I took the bus back home. Mom was glad I was back but not dad. I felt like a wimp, even after waking up.

Chapter 3

When Owen was ready that morning, we took off in his Renault to Pauls Valley. The sky had cleared up, and it was sunny.

We stopped along the way at a McDonald's for breakfast. The sign heralded: Home of fifteen-cent Hamburgers.

"We're home," Owen said as we approached a small ranch-style house. A string of white Christmas lights draped across the red brick facade, a wreath hung on the green door, and a white picket fence provided the border in the front lawn. There were a few rose bushes to the right of the house.

Owen rang the bell.

"Come on in, come on in," an elderly man said, opening the door. The bells on the Christmas wreath jingled. The man was wearing dark-brown corduroy pants, a white shirt, and a cardigan. I guessed he was Owen's dad. "Who do we have here?"

It was a relief to step out of the cold into the warm house. As Owen introduced me, a matronly blond woman, wearing horn-rimmed glasses, walked in from a door to the right.

"I heard voices and thought it must be you," she said, hugging Owen.

Owen returned the hug and gestured to me. "Mom, this is Ashley. He's from Phoenix."

She asked if we had eaten lunch. We said we did.

"Come in, come in, anyways," she said as she walked toward the kitchen, and we followed her.

Once inside she pointed to a small round table.

"You must be hungry after all that driving. You should eat something. It's a long time to dinner, with the party and all." She placed two small plates with apple pie and ice cream on top in front of us. Owen's dad had come in and was standing close to us. He started telling us what Owen's sister Dana wanted for the party and who was invited.

We heard the front door open and the voices of two girls. Soon they came in, dressed in Wrangler Jeans and winter jackets. Their hands were full of packages, decorations, and stuff.

"Hi, Sis," Owen said. "Need any help?"

"Hey. When did you get in?"

"Just a while ago."

Dana didn't even look at me, but asked if Owen could help her get stuff from the car. I offered to help, but they said to just sit back and relax. I was stuck with Owen's dad, not knowing what to talk about. After a while I excused myself and went down to the basement where Owen was helping Dana put up the decorations. I joined them.

Chapter 4

There were ten people at the party, more girls than boys.

"You know all these people?" I whispered, turning to Owen.

"Not really," he said.

Dana came and pulled him to other corner of the room. The punch bowl needed to be filled. I kept looking around, finding nothing to do.

"Hi," I heard someone calling me in a high-pitched voice.

I turned. A beaming, buxom girl in a tight-fitting red dress was standing within a foot of me. She was wearing a lot of perfume, which I didn't like. Not knowing what to say, I just kept looking at her, a bit embarrassed. All dressed up for the party, she looked pretty.

"Haven't seen you around here. You with someone?" she said.

"Uh, no, well, yes," I stuttered, not knowing the best way to continue the conversation. It was times like this when I hated myself. It wasn't the first time I'd attended a dance party. But here I was among high-school kids. How does one talk with high-school kids?

"I'm with Owen. I'm his roommate at college," I finally said.

"Oh, a college guy," she said, and walked away.

What was that about? Did I insult her? *You are a dummy, Ashley. You didn't even get her name. You got a chance to get acquainted with a nice girl, and you blew it. Maybe I should follow her and ask her if I did something wrong?* But it was probably too late for that.

I stood at the back of the room watching everyone else enjoy the party since I didn't know anyone and didn't want to look too pushy. A while later I tried to weave through the dancing couples to get to the punch bowl and crackers. Owen was nowhere around.

I filled a plastic cup with punch, placed some chips and crackers on a paper plate, and tried to return to where I had been standing at the back of the room, but some kids had taken my place. The other option was to go to the corner near the stairs. It was difficult to balance the plastic cup full of punch and a small paper plate as I moved between the people, pulling my shoulders up to avoid bumping into someone. It didn't help. Someone bumped into me anyway. Before I could say "I'm sorry," the punch was on my pants. I raised my arms and looked down. It looked like I had peed on my pants, and everything from paper plate was on the floor.

What a bumbling fool, I thought. I looked around to see if anyone noticed.

The girl who had walked away from me earlier was looking at me and smiling.

"Don't be such a prude; go on and dance." It was Owen's mom pushing me into the crowd, gyrating to the tunes of "Sugar Pie Honey Bunch." I was red in my face.

I joined the crowd, managing to leave the plate and the cup in a corner. Another girl faced me, weaving her arms and body in a smooth left and right motion. I tried to mimic her, but I knew I was making a spectacle.

I was glad when the music stopped.

"Having a good time?" It was Owen. I managed to say yes. I was lying. I tried to wipe my face.

"Let's get out of here," he said, pointing toward the stairs. Finally relief.

His dad was sitting on a plaid sofa. He enquired about how I was doing at the college. I told him about meeting Owen and how worried I was about finding a room.

"Have faith in *him.* He will take care of everything," he said, pointing his fingers to the ceiling.

I nodded.

We started back to Norman the next day after breakfast.

Owen's mom had made scrambled eggs, bacon, and pancake
thanked them for their hospitality as we walked toward Owen's
car. His father waved at us from the front door and called out,
"God Bless."

.

Chapter 5

We didn't talk much as we drove back. The normally talkative Owen was quiet. I wondered why? Was he upset by my behavior at the party? I really didn't do anything to embarrass him. As we approached the campus, he finally spoke.

"Want to go to the school cafeteria for lunch?" he asked.

"Yes," I replied.

He parked his car in the parking lot of his dorm. As we walked out, he noticed that the car was not aligned properly in the parking lanes.

"Just a minute," he said as he opened the driver side door and got in. I saw him turn the ignition key but the car did not start. After several attempts, he gave up.

"Damn it," he said. "I don't know what's wrong. I just changed the battery. Could be the alternator. If that's the case we are doomed. It may take several days to get the parts for this foreign car."

"Don't worry. It'll work out," I said, even though I wasn't sure what was involved in getting the part. I had to say something to console him.

"I do worry. I had promised to take you around to look for a room. Now I can't," he said.

"It's not the end of the world."

"Shit, man," Owen stamped his foot.

We walked for about fifteen minutes to the cafeteria. I had no idea where we were going. I simply followed him. A few students were walking around. Past the building that had *Department of Physics* etched on the top, stood a smaller building. A door to the side led us to the cafeteria. We each picked up a tray and walked along the counter. I was impressed by the long stretch of food—from salads, main dishes to desserts. I never would have thought a college cafeteria offered so much food. I wondered who the caterer was.

Owen met some of his classmates. They talked about the OU football schedule and whether OU would beat UT. I was aware of the intense rivalry between Oklahoma University and the University of Texas. But I couldn't participate in the conversation much because I wasn't familiar with the players.

The lunch and the time with his friends calmed Owen down.

"Let's go over to the Student's Union," he said with a smile. "There's a message board there with notices for room rentals."

"Good idea. That'll give me a head start tomorrow."

Chapter 6

The message board did have notices with tear off pieces
with addresses. I tore off a few. On our way back, we stopped at
the Sunoco gas station and picked up a street map of Norman.
That night Owen marked addresses on the map to make it easier
for me to follow.

The next day I got up early and told Owen not to wait for
me for breakfast, since his priority was to get his car fixed. I
stopped by at the Rickner's again. There was a different waitress
this time. I ordered a doughnut and coffee. The first address was
within a block to the right. The Rooms for Rent sign was
prominent. I knocked on the door.

"Yes?" a man asked as he opened the door.

"I'm looking for a room. I saw your sign."

"Sorry. All taken," he said, and closed the door on me.

What was that all about? Was it my looks? Did I look like a
dangerous criminal out to rob him? Did I look like a hobo? I
thought people in the South were known for their hospitality. Why
couldn't he be polite at least? Well, what can you do?

The second address was bit far. I stopped by a lamppost

and read the map to see if there was a shortcut. I saw a man walking toward me with his dog. I was hesitant to talk to him after the experience just a few minutes ago.

"Are you looking for something?" he asked.

"Yes."

I showed him the mark on the map.

"Make a left at the next block, then a right after two blocks. You'll be right there."

I thanked him. Not all men are assholes.

It was cold by Phoenix standards, and I was feeling it on my face and ears. The wind made it worse. I kept rubbing my hands. My fingers were numb even with gloves on. Sometimes I pushed them inside the pockets of my overcoat.

"Hello, young man. What can I do for you?" Again a middle-aged man answered the door at the second house. He looked friendly, but I wondered how he would react.

After I told him why I was there, he asked where I was from.

"I would have no problem renting a room to you, young man. But can you get a guarantee from someone? I'm not saying you wouldn't be able to pay the rent, but I can't take chances."

"I have an assistantship. I'll get a stipend."

"Fine! But I need to see the letter or something in writing."

"I don't have it with me right now."

"Well then, come back when you have it, okay?"

At least he didn't slam the door on me. I wouldn't blame him for having doubts about an out-of-towner.

No one answered at the next two addresses. All the walking had resulted in nothing. I wished I had called these places before coming but thought it was better to talk to people in person. It had started to snow a bit, just a few flurries. It was a thrilling experience for me. I spread my arms wide and looked up at the sky. The flakes on my face were refreshing. I knew I had walked quite a ways from the campus. It was past noon, and I was getting hungry. My toes and fingers were getting numb.

Is this what growing up is supposed to be? Independence? Oh, yeah. I wanted to prove myself. To be accepted as an adult. That's what I had told my mom. I wasn't a kid anymore.

There was not a restaurant or café in sight. I had to get inside, somewhere, or else I would freeze and wouldn't be able to walk. But where? I didn't know the town.

I kept walking. I felt something in my pants pocket. I reached inside with my gloved hand. I had forgotten that I had kept some lifesavers and Kit Kats with me. It was small consolation, but I still needed to eat something. I realized I was on a main street from the traffic, more cars, commercial vehicles, and vans. A bus turned into a small building. Then I remembered that this was the bus station where I'd gotten off two days ago. I knew they had a small lunch counter.

It was past two in the afternoon when I finished my lunch at the bus-station lunch counter. I dreaded stepping out in the cold weather again. I still had two more locations to check out. It would start getting dark soon. I looked at the map and started walking. I noticed a mailman delivering mail in one block. So, there was someone else to give me company on these deserted streets. A UPS van was parked in front of another house.

I knocked on the door of the next house on my list. A young man wearing sweatpants and matching hoodie answered. He asked me to wait and went inside to get the owner, whose name I later learned was Mrs. English. She came out with a smiling face. In a grandmotherly tone, she said she had a room to rent but was holding it for another young man who was going to confirm by that evening.

"Come back tomorrow, and I'll know for sure," she said.

I thanked her and said I would do that.

"Will it be all right if I call you?"

"Of course."

She gave me her number.

At least there was a glimmer of hope for me, only a hope. What if the other boy takes it? What if there are no more rooms left at the last house on my list? I am doomed. One more day and I will have to move out of Owen's dorm. God! Oh God, please help me.

I was approaching the main campus. As I walked I noticed a colonial house to my right. It had a long porch with steps leading up to it. There was a swing to the right and two rocking chairs to the left of the steps. A long concrete driveway to the right of the house stretched up to a detached garage. I stopped to allow a Chevy Impala turn into the driveway. An elderly woman got out of the driver's side. She had a cane in one hand and took a while to come out. She opened the trunk, looked inside, and then looked at the steps.

"Do you need any help, ma'am?" I asked timidly.

"Oh, hi there. You a student at the university?"

Her tone was friendly and reminded me of my grandma.

"Yes, ma'am."

She looked at me from head to toe.

"Well, you look like a nice fella. Sure, if you don't mind doing so. I was going to call Andy next door, but since you're here I will accept your offer."

"No problem." I guessed Andy mowed her lawn or something in summer or helped her out otherwise.

I picked up two of the grocery bags, one in each hand, and waited for her to walk up the steps slowly and unlock the door. As I followed her to the kitchen, she said to leave the bags on the breakfast table.

"I'll put them in later; let them be here for now," she said. She sat on the chair and took a long breath.

I went outside and brought the remaining two bags.

"You take care. I'll be leaving now," I said as I waited by the kitchen door.

"Well, don't leave yet. You've been such a nice boy. Take a seat. I'll fix you some hot chocolate."

"I don't want to bother you, ma'am. I should be going."

"Oh, no, no bother at all. It's so cold outside and looks like you've been walking. I can see from your red cheeks. Sit."

The hot drink really perked me up.

"So, are you a new student here?" she asked.

I told her that I was from out of town and about my unsuccessful attempts to look for a room.

"You know that you remind me of my youngest son Tommy, so much," she said in her soft voice, taking a sip from her drink and looking at the tabletop dreamily.

"Yes," she continued. "It's been a year and half. He's all the way to the other side of the world serving his draft in this damn war."

I could see tears swelling up in her eyes. "I'm sorry," I said.

She recounted that her husband of thirty-five years passed

away two years ago from complications of prostate cancer. Her elder daughter was living in Illinois, and her other son was working in San Diego.

"They are living their own lives, you know."

She kept quiet for a few minutes, and then looked out the kitchen window.

She turned to me and continued, "I'll let you stay in Tommy's room until you find a permanent place or longer if you wish. You've been so good."

"That's nice of you, ma'am. I don't even know your name," I said.

"Abigail. Most people call me Abi."

"Thank you for your offer, Abi," I hesitated to call her by her name. I was used to addressing elderly people as Mr. or Mrs. "But I can't live like a freeloader."

"No, don't think of it that way. Look, I'm staying here alone. You can help with some household chores when needed."

"What would I owe you?"

"Look. When Tommy left for the war, I was renting his room. I did it for a year and then stopped. This is a university town. We trust people. What can you afford?"

"What if I pay you thirty dollars a month, and I'll still help you when you need it?"

"Oh, my! You're so gracious. That's a deal. Go get your stuff, and God bless you."

I raised my fingers to the sky as I looked up and then touched my heart stepping down the stoop outside. I was happy the way everything turned out. I was relieved and smiled as I reached Owen's dorm.

Ashok Shenolikar

**Part 2
Owen
1967**

Ashok Shenolikar

Chapter 7

"We'll be landing soon. Please fasten your seat belts."

It is the pilot making an announcement. I open my eyes, sit upright, and look out the airplane window. The plane has started to descend, and it is low enough for me to see the ground below. The bright sunlight displays small city streets, mini vans, and buses on unpaved roads spewing clouds of dirt. People walk along the streets with bundles on their head. An occasional ox cart makes its way forward slowly. The land looks plush with trees, water on one side and mountains on the other side, and for a moment, it feels like being in Florida, if it weren't for the mountains. I have reached Lilongwe, Malawi, Africa, on my mission to be a Peace Corps Volunteer. It's going to be a culture shock for me—a new country, people alien in looks as well as mode of living, and a language completely different than English. Am I going to survive? What will happen if I get sick or don't like the food? I haven't the faintest idea. When I was serving in Vietnam, we followed orders without thinking. We moved together in a platoon and established close bonds. We cried when someone died in combat. I hope to have a challenging experience here and maybe find new friends.

We, eight boys and two girls, all in our early twenties, walk out of the airplane into a small airport. A summer-like hot breeze blows past our faces as we wait outside the baggage carousel for our coordinator, Cameron. He arrives soon to receive us.

"Welcome to Malawi," he says. "I know you all are tired after the long flight and want to rest, but bear with me for a while. We'll go to the orientation center where I'll brief you about where you'll be staying and the rest of the program for the coming weeks."

Cameron leaves to get the transportation. Our luggage is piled up behind us. That's when I notice a young girl dressed in jeans and a pullover looking around the luggage with eyebrows crinkled and frowning. *Go help the distressed girl*, a voice in me says.

"May I help you? Lost something?" I say, approaching her. I jump over a piece of luggage and land right next to her. She looks so innocent and vulnerable with her pale white face and troubled looks.

"Oh, it's right here. Shoot. I was so worried," she says picking up a backpack. Turning to me, she adds, "I'm sorry. You were saying?"

"You looked like you lost something."

"I couldn't see my backpack. It's right here. Thanks."

"No problem. See you later."

Her ponytail bounces as she walks. When the van comes, we drive a short distance to the Peace Corps briefing center. I want to sit close to "the girl" and get to know her, but she has already taken a seat in the front, right behind the driver.

Cameron starts to brief. "Each of you will stay with a host family during the preservice training," he says. "Staying with the locals is part of the assimilation with the Malawi culture. At the end of the training, you will be assigned to locations where you will stay for the duration of your assignment."

I am to stay with the Aguda family, who live in the Northwest part of the city. I want to know where "the girl" is going to stay, but miss or don't understand what was said.

The Peace Corps doesn't waste any time. The three-month preservice training starts the next day. The classes cover various topics, including technical, cross-culture awareness, local language, personal health, and safety.

I spot "the girl" sitting in the second row. The long floral dress makes her look slim. I want to talk with her but am not sure the best way to do it. *Maybe I should wait for an appropriate moment.* At one point she turns her head toward me and I half raise my hand to say hello, but she has already looked away. I am not sure if she remembers me from the airport incident.

At the break I walk up closer to her and say, "Hi."

"Hi," she replies.

"I'm Owen. Remember me?"

"Yes, I do. You're the one who offered to help me yesterday? That was nice of you."

"Thanks. And you are?" I ask.

"Rachel."

"Nice to meet you, Rachel."

I don't know why I feel so happy talking to Rachel. It's time for us to get back to our seats. Spotting an empty seat, I move over and sit next to her.

"You mind?" I ask before sitting.

"No. Go ahead," she says with a smile, which I like.

I reflect on my days in Pauls Valley. I dated a few girls growing up there, and when I was a student at the university in Norman. None was as beautiful or appeared to be as mature and charismatic as Rachel.

Chapter 8

Mr. and Mrs. Aguda live in a small house with mud walls and corrugated tin roof. It has three rooms. The bathroom is a small square shield with open roof with no plumbing or shower. I quickly learn to take bath with water heated on a wood stove and brought in a plastic bucket. I sit on the floor and pour hot water over my head with a tumbler. Cameron advised us during the initial briefing to buy a pee bucket, bug killer, and pot scrubber. I wash my clothes by hand and hang them to dry on a clothesline outside.

I take breakfast with the Aguda family every day before going to the training. Mr. Aguda is a teacher and speaks good English.

In the evenings, when I am alone in my assigned room, I play my guitar or read one of the books I brought with me. But I can't get Rachel out of my mind. *What is she doing now?* I don't have her telephone number, and I don't know where she is staying so I can't talk with her or walk to her place and spend time with her.

"It's not safe to walk around by yourself, especially at night," we were told during the first day's briefing.

.

Chapter 9

One day Rachel tells me where she is staying. It's a fifteen-minute walk from Mr. Aguda's house. I sit next to her whenever I can. She doesn't seem to mind. Slowly I come to know a bit about her family.

"Dad's a professor of American history, and Mom's an elementary school teacher. I miss them," she says.

"Do you write to them often?" I ask.

"When I find time. It takes almost a month to get their response."

"Yeah. I wish there was a faster way to communicate. Making an international call is such a hassle."

"I know what you mean."

She doesn't ask me about my family. I want to take her out somewhere but am not familiar with the town.

"What's a good place to visit around here?" I ask Mr. Aguda one evening. We were already in the second month of our three-month training.

"What do you have in mind?" he asks.

"Nothing in particular. It's just that I was thinking of

taking a girl in our class to an interesting place. We could get to see more of the town and learn about the culture."

He smiles.

"You've a girlfriend already?" he asks after a pause.

"We're just friends."

"I understand," he says. "Our town's not very big. There's the Old Town, and there's the City Center. The City Center is mostly offices and embassies. I think you'll like the Old Town with its market. There's shopping, small stores, and restaurants. It's a busy place. I heard you playing your guitar. You'll like the Malawian music. I should warn you about pickpockets, however. You don't look like us. You need to be extra careful."

"Thanks, Mr. Aguda," I say.

"And, please don't walk the streets after dark."

"Yes. We were warned about that. Thank you again."

.

Chapter 10

Next day I ask Rachel if she is interested in visiting the Old Town that weekend.

"Oh, I'd love that," she says.

The Old Town is like a flea market in the United States. Small individual stores, adjacent to each other, sell produce stacked in heaps on wooden tables or spread out on the floor in large wooden bowls. Some sell live chickens, fish, and colorful clothes. A lady displays wooden carvings and jewelry spread on a cloth on the ground. A busy road with vans, buses going back and forth, and people walking every which way is to one side of the market. Young boys and girls push handmade necklaces and knickknacks at us. We don't understand what they are saying. I have to hold Rachel's hand lest we get separated in the crowd. It is hard to hear each other with the calypso-like music blaring from the speakers in some stores. Rachel is pulling me in every direction like a child in an amusement park.

"Let's go in here," she says, pointing to a small clothing store. It's little more than a tent with clothes hung on racks. A lady, dressed in native clothes, approaches us and starts showing the clothes. We have to manage with sign language.

"How does this look?" Rachel asks. She has draped a green-and-purple scarf around her shoulders.

"You look very pretty," I say.

"Be serious." She makes a serious face.

"I am. The colors are perfect. You look radiant."

"You're too much."

We both smile. She doesn't buy it.

We have been walking for two hours greeting passersby with a nod and a smile. We have practiced some Chichewa words to say "hello" *(Moni)* or "how're you" *(Muli Bwanji)*. They smile and respond with the wave of their hand.

We don't know how far we have come from the center. It's also late in the afternoon.

"Would you like to get a bite and a drink?" I ask Rachel.

"I think that would be nice," she says.

There is a low-roofed building facing us. The Sanctuary Lodge says the sign.

"Why don't we go in here?" she suggests.

As we enter we are greeted by a tall man, dressed in black trousers, white shirt, and tie. He escorts us to a table in a corner. Fortunately he speaks English, but with a bit of an accent. The rustic surroundings and minimal decorations give a soft feeling about the place. Overhead fans whirl providing a breeze. Each table has candles providing dim light.

"Very romantic," I say. "You had a good hunch."

She smiles.

Chapter 11

"You haven't told me much about yourself," Rachel says as we are seated.

I tell her about Pauls Valley, my tour of duty in Viet Nam, and my love for running and playing guitar.

"You're a guitar player? Get out of here," she says in mock surprise.

"Yes. I mean, not professionally."

"Still, I'd like to hear you play sometime."

"I'll play for you when we are settled in our assignments."

"Do you know when they'll tell us?"

The waiter approaches and wants to know if we are ready to order. We haven't even looked at the menu.

"Take your time. I'll be back soon."

The restaurant has local Malawian food, the *Nsima*, as well as chicken, meatballs, and steak. Plenty of choices. When the waiter returns we order.

"Have you eaten food like this? African food?" I ask.

"Not really, but I want to try. Hope I don't get sick."

"Why would you?"

"Well, my stomach acts funny sometimes, you may say. Especially when I eat something I'm not used to."

"You'll be okay. Let's enjoy the moment."

"Do you know when they'll let us know where we'll be stationed?" Rachel brings up the subject again.

The waiter has brought our food. He places it in front of us as he adjusts the settings.

"Enjoy," he says, and leaves us alone.

"I heard it will be on the last day of training," I say.

"Wouldn't it be nice if we both get the same town?" Rachel says.

I'm glad Rachel spoke what was on my mind.

"I agree. We shall see," I say.

We take a taxi back to her place, as it is getting dark. I sit close to her. We continue talking. She likes Barbara Streisand and the Bond movies. The taxi drops us a few feet from her place. As we walk to the front door, I have my hands around her waist.

"I had a great time. Thanks for the dinner too," Rachel says as we face each other.

"Me too. It was good to get out."

She starts to walk toward the door. I hesitate a bit, but then pull her toward me. I feel her soft bosom against my chest and her warm breath as I kiss her lightly. She doesn't resist.

"Good night," she says turning toward me as I watch her open the door.

"Good night," I say, adding, "we should do it again."

She smiles one last time before closing the door. I wave and start walking back toward Mr. Aguda's house. I am defying the warnings not to walk alone. I decide to do it anyway. *I'm a man, and I can run fast.* A couple of boys cross me, but nothing happens. They are talking loudly in their dialect and ignore me. I sleep well that night.

Chapter 12

On the last day of the preservice training, we learn that I am going to be volunteering in Zomba and Rachel in Blantyre, thirty-five miles away. It means I am not going to see her every day, nor talk with her since there were no telephones in the huts where we are going to stay. I frown but resolve to continue our friendship. I don't want to lose Rachel.

Chapter 13

My home for the next two years is going to be in the Malemia village, Zomba. It's a two-room mud cottage with a thatched roof. The entrance is through a wooden door with a latch and a large padlock with key. It is furnished with a small bed, a stove, and a small table with two plastic chairs in the kitchen. A kerosene lantern serves as light. There's a tap outside, to be shared with other neighbors, serving as a source of water, a shield under the open sky to take a bath and a pit latrine with no flush button.

"Here we are. Just settle down, and I'll come and get you tomorrow and show you our clinic," Kasigo says as she prepares to leave. Kasigo is the nurse in the village clinic and my mentor. She promises to introduce me to the village chief in time.

"Thanks. Looking forward," I say before realizing that I said the same thing the previous night when she had received me at the drop-off point.

I dump my bag, guitar, and my backpack on the mud floor. I look around. *So be it*, I say to myself.

"Don't expect to stay in a four-star hotel," the Peace Corps managers said. "You've got to immerse yourselves with the locals, live with them, eat their food, and help them in whatever way you can to better their lives." We were trained in the local customs and a few local words, which I forgot. We were told not to flaunt anything American. I wondered if my white skin would be a source of novelty to my neighbors, and I wasn't sure what their reaction would be.

I didn't have much to unpack. I look around the room once more when I hear someone whispering and giggling close to me. I turn around and find four children, all half naked, observing my every move. The front door was left open. It's very hot and humid outside, like mid-August in Las Vegas. I walk over and say, "Hello." They just smile. They probably have never seen a white man up close. They point to a young man sitting on a wooden bench outside an adjacent cottage. A while later he walks over to us.

"Welcome to our village," he says in English. He says his name is Ayo, and he's a student at the local school and has learned English.

Chapter 14

Ayo is to be my local guide. He takes me for a walk in the neighborhood. There is a market where street vendors sell vegetables and fruit spread out on mats or cloth on the street. A small brick room with tin roof sells groceries, toiletries, and other small stuff.

It is getting close to evening, and women have started grinding corn in a stone grinder outside their cottages. Our cottages are huddled together. I stand near one cottage and watch as the corn paste is molded into patties to make the *Nsima*. I quickly learn that corn is a staple food for the Malawians. Only those who can afford it eat fish and chicken. On a stove made out of three stones and using wood for fire, they are preparing a sauce in a large pot. It smells like vegetable soup. A lady talks with Ayo in the local dialect, which I don't understand.

"She's asking if you would like to join them for dinner," he says.

I agree.

I see chickens trotting the compound and sheep grazing the grass. The place smells of stale garbage. A while later the man of the house walks in after the day's work. I learn he has two wives.

We wash our hands in a common bowl before eating. I don't know how clean it is. I don't like the taste of the *Nsima* but eat it anyway. I thank the family and return to my cottage.

Chapter 15

The next day I walk to the health clinic where Kasigo works. The day is sunny and has started to warm up. Even at the early hour, men and women have lined up outside the three-room clinic. Some are squatting on the floor and others are standing— waiting for their turn to be called in.

Kasigo welcomes and tells me that I am to help her manage and plan for the distribution of medicines throughout her jurisdiction.

"Our village has so many health issues," she says.

"Yes. I read about it," I say.

"There's malaria, AIDS, malnutrition, large families," she continues. "There's only so much we can do, you know."

"You're right. Tell me how I can be of help."

I spend the rest of the day helping Kasigo take inventory of the medical supplies. A large quantity of mosquito nets is on order, and they have to be distributed throughout the village.

While all this is going on, I have little time to think of

Rachel. I want to know how she is adjusting and what she has to do. I know she is in a village close to Blantyre but don't know where or how to get in touch with her. There is no telephone in my cottage, and I think it is the same with her.

Chapter 16

On my first day off, I decide to travel to Blantyre to meet Rachel. Kasigo informs me of my options—share a minibus or take the government bus. The latter option is cheaper. The bus depot is crowded, a bit chaotic. Men approach me with in-your-face offers of a ride to Blantyre. I ignore them and go to where the bus is parked. The bus doesn't leave on time, which I am told later is very common.

On reaching Blantyre, I go straight to the local Peace Corps office. They tell me Rachel is staying in the Goliati village at the outskirts of the town. There is no address. I take a taxi, which leaves me in the vicinity. I am hoping she is home. But how am I going to find her cottage? There are children playing in courtyards. Some women just stare at me with a blank expression as they sweep their courtyards with a hand broom made out of thatch or grind corn to prepare the meal.

"American? American?" I keep asking, waving my hand.

Finally a teenage girl speaks in broken English and points to a hut. It is similar to mine. I knock on the door. An American girl, but not Rachel, opens the door. She introduces herself as Agnes and says she is a volunteer worker for USAID.

"I'm looking for a PC volunteer," I say.

"Is her name Rachel by any chance?" Agnes asks.

"Yes."

Agnes says Rachel lives a few blocks away, but I wouldn't find her there.

"What's going on?" I ask.

"I took her to the Peace Corps infirmary in Blantyre this morning. She got sick from something she ate. Want to know how to go there?"

"I'd appreciate that."

Chapter 17

I find Rachel lying on a bed in the infirmary. She looks tired. I give her a hug.

"What did you do to yourself?" I ask.

"It's the local food," Rachel says. "I thought I would get to like it, but my stomach just couldn't take it. When I pooped in my pants, I knew I needed help."

I remembered her saying that in Lilongwe.

"How long are they going to keep you here?"

"Until I get better."

"Hope it's not too long."

"I hope so too."

We talk about our assignments. Rachel is teaching English in a secondary school. She has to wait and take a breather before she can continue talking.

"How're you managing it?" I ask.

"The kids are great, but the facility needs a lot."

"How so?"

"Well, there aren't any tables and chairs. Kids sit on the floor."

She coughs as she talks. I get up and fetch a glass of water. We talk about our living conditions. Rachel tells me she has cockroaches running around in her kitchen and she hates it. She doesn't want to cook in that place. I say my place isn't any better, but maybe we will get used to it.

It's getting late, and I have to return to Zomba. There is no guarantee when the last bus will be. I want to stay with Rachel and help her until she gets better, but I need to get back to Zomba for my duties.

"You take care," I say as I get up to leave. "I'll be back again as soon as I can. You call me if you need anything." I give her a hug and the number of Kasigo's clinic.

"Thanks for coming. Really appreciate it." She turns on her side as I take one last glance through the door. *Poor girl*, I say. I am worried about her.

Chapter 18

I am adjusting to my life in the village. I have learned to cook small meals, mostly eggs and vegetables. Writing letters back home is a chore. It takes four to five weeks to get a response. Mom keeps sending recipes, but all I have here is a kerosene stove and a couple of pots. I enjoy the occasional packages of chocolate and cookies from home. Dad, sometimes, gives updates on President Johnson's great society initiative. At night I sit out on the stoop playing my guitar. Kids gather around me to listen. It's hot. The mosquitoes whizz past my face when I sit outside and even inside when sleeping. I have learned to ignore an occasional mouse running across the floor and spiders and lizards trotting on the walls.

I want to be with Rachel, but the only way I can do it is when I visit her. The volunteers have no telephones. I can send letters locally but there is no guarantee that they'll be delivered. I am helping Kasigo plan several health projects.

"We need to educate the people, Kasigo," I say.

"It's true, but most of our people can't read."

"We can have small meetings in the market or in our clinic. We can draw pictures, and talk to them about how to keep their houses and surroundings clean. Tell them about how mosquitoes breed and how not to let water accumulate near their huts. There is so much we can do."

"You would help me do all that? What if they don't come? Men are busy working in their fields, and women are busy cooking, washing clothes, and taking care of the many children."

"We can try and see what happens." I want to convince her.

Chapter 19

When I go for my morning run and see families with multiple children, I think about ways to teach these people about planning their families, about birth control. What if it goes against their religion or lifelong community norms? Is talking about these issues a taboo here?

I don't have easy answers.

At the clinic local people are uneasy talking with a white man. Kasigo talks to them in the native language, interpreting my words.

One evening I am sitting on the stoop in my courtyard playing my guitar. I see Ayo running toward me.

"Mr. Owen, Mr. Owen, come with me fast, please," he says.

I'm puzzled. What could be happening?

"Ayo, what's wrong?" I ask.

"Come please. Baako is very sick."

"But Ayo, I'm not a doctor."

"But you're American. You'll know what to do."

I follow him two huts over. Baako is a teenager. He's lying on the floor on a mat. His parents are squatting next to him. Four other children are playing in the dirt outside, unaware of what's going on. I touch his forehead. He's hot. I'm sure he has a high fever. It could be due to malaria or an infection. I don't know. I go to my hut and bring aspirin with me. I feed him two tablets with water. I'm not sure how clean the water is. I tell Baako's parents to boil the water before drinking. Ayo is my interpreter.

"Let's see what happens," I say to Ayo. "In the morning bring him to the clinic and let Kasigo check him." I'm not sure if what I did is going to work.

The next morning I ask Kasigo if Baako made it to the clinic.

"Yes. I think there is not much we can do here. He needs to go the hospital in the city."

"Will he do it?"

"I'm not sure. That's the problem we have here. Most people don't have the money to go to the city and also pay the doctor's fee."

"Can I help?"

"No. It's not your responsibility. Something will come up."

"I hope so."

Chapter 20

It's been a month since I last saw Rachel in the infirmary. She hasn't called. One weekend I take the bus again to Blantyre to meet her. It is a one-hour ride, but it seems longer since the bus doesn't start on time. It also makes several stops to pick up passengers, and before I know it, it's packed. At every stop, vendors bang on the windows of the bus to sell their wares— photos of the city and animals seen in a safari.

I wish I had taken a taxi or one of the mini buses instead of the state-run bus. But I have to budget my expense to survive on the meager Peace Corps allowance. The roads are bumpy, and some passengers are carrying live chickens in the bus. I cover my nose to avoid inhaling the dust and the smell. I'm the only white person among a bus load of black faces. Some stare at me and observe my every move.

Rachel gives me a close hug and I kiss her on the cheek.

"Feeling better?" I ask.

"Yes, much better."

I can feel that just by looking at her smiling face.

"Let's celebrate."

"What would you like to do?"

"Let's go to the city and have some fun."

"I'd love that."

We take a taxi to Blantyre. I have heard of the Mandela House, home of the *La Caverna* Art Gallery, and café. The taxi drops us in the vicinity. We barely look at the artifacts. We are so happy to be with each other. We walk slowly looking at some paintings but soon lose interest in the gallery. It's past lunch time. The place is not busy. We walk over to the onsite restaurant.

I notice Rachel has been quiet for some time. I ask if everything is all right, whether her stomach virus is acting up again.

"I got a letter from my mom," she says. "Little Shane will be playing in a high-school musical."

"That's great." I try to encourage her.

"But don't you realize that I can't be there. I miss him so much."

"Oh. I'm sorry." I realize I didn't say the right thing.

"I'm sorry you can't be there is what I mean," I clarify.

I think she is going to cry. I put my arms around her. I want to ask who Shane is. Is it her brother? It can't be her son if he is in high school. Rachel is about my age, in midtwenties.

"Oh, how I wish I was back home," Rachel says again, almost choking, her voice guttural.

"I hope you asked them to take a lot of pictures," I say. I know it doesn't matter what I say, it isn't going to help.

Rachel continues to talk about her family. It is the first time she has opened up.

"We used to watch the *Lucy Show* and *Gomer Pyle* together and laugh our hearts out." Rachel continues. Still no clue as to who Shane is.

"When Shane was born, I was six years old, and Mom decided to stay home for a while," she continues.

Now I figure Shane is her younger brother.

We finish our lunch and return to Rachel's place. Rachel hasn't said a word during the ride. I think it is better to leave her alone.

"So, I'll take the evening bus back to Zomba," I say.

Rachel says okay with a sad face as if she doesn't care what I do. She doesn't even look at me. I think some alone time will allow her to come back to normal.

Chapter 21

I'm getting tired of taking the bus to Blantyre. I wish Rachel would come to Zomba sometimes. We could go trekking along the mountains. But that never happens.

"Mr. Owen, my brother Ebo works at a motorbike repair shop," Kasigo says one day. "He knows someone who wants to sell his moped. You interested?"

I mentally count the money I have saved.

"Sure," I reply. A moped would give me mobility and allow me to visit Rachel more often. Although it may take some practice weaving through the traffic on the dirt roads and competing with cars, mini buses, and walkers by the side of the road. Still, I am excited.

I buy the moped for one hundred dollars, half of my monthly allowance.

One Friday I finish my work early. I want to surprise Rachel by showing up at her school on my new vehicle. The school is a one-level rectangular brick building with tin roof and two windows opposite each other and no front door. Students are sitting on the floor. Rachel is teaching a class. I wave at her and wait outside until she is finished. Two children follow her.

"This is Eza, and this is Gamba," Rachel says pointing to the two boys who accompany her. They are not quite teenagers yet.

"Hi there," I say. "You like your teacher?"

"Yes." Eza and Gamba answer together in a soft voice while looking at the floor.

I don't want to miss the moment. I take out my Kodak instamatic.

"Why don't you both stand here," I say to Eza and Gamba, pointing next to Rachel.

I take a picture of Rachel and her students. Then I stand next to her and ask Eza to take our picture. Eza holds the camera with both hands extended straight ahead of him and clicks and immediately gives it back to me as if he is afraid of damaging it. Eza and Gamba stand close to Rachel and me, admiring the camera and the whole picture taking session.

"What do we have here?" Rachel asks approaching my moped.

"Want to go for a ride?"

"Cool."

We drive to Blantyre and have dinner at a not-so-expensive

Chinese diner.

"You aren't going to be sick with this food, are you?" I ask.

"I hope not. Normally I'm fine with Chinese food. It's the African food that I have problems with."

We eat leisurely and return to her hut after two hours. It is late in the evening and getting dark.

"Will you stay here overnight? It would be much safer to ride back in the morning." Rachel suggests. I agree.

Chapter 22

I realize I haven't written to my parents in a while. In an earlier letter Dad informed me that he had retired and was volunteering as an events planner at the Pauls Valley church. I don't know why I think of my friend Ashley Wilkins from Oklahoma University. I look through my contact list and find his address at the University of Michigan where he started as an assistant professor. I write letters to my parents and to Ashley. I enclose copies of my picture with Rachel. *We are just friends*, I write.

I've been here for almost a year and a half now. There are six more months before I finish my duty as a Peace Corps Volunteer.

"Mr. Owen, we have the mosquito nets finally," Kasigo says one day.

"Weren't they ordered when I came here?"

"Yes. This is Africa. That's the way it is."

We make plans to visit the families in the village to distribute the nets. It's a challenge to teach them how to tie the nets over their beds. Most sleep on the floor on mats. Some families are large with six to eight children. But maybe we have to prioritize based on a family's situation.

One such family is the Ibori family. Mr. Akua Ibori and his wife Bayo have three children, and Bayo is pregnant again. Their eldest son, Demond, left school to help out his father in his maize farm. I am sorry that we can give them only one net. I hope that the mosquito net will make the mother's life a bit bearable, especially during her pregnancy.

A couple of months go by.

"Mrs. Ibori gave birth to a baby girl," Kasigo tells me as I enter the clinic. It's a beautiful day, and I am planning to go to the village market and stock up on the groceries after work.

"How're mother and the baby?" I ask.

"Mother is okay, but the baby didn't survive," Kasigo says, as if it was a regular event.

"How did that happen? I'm sorry to hear that."

"She probably didn't sleep under the net and got infected. There was no net. It was stolen within two days after we gave it to them."

"What? Who would do a thing like that?"

"It's a problem we have," Kogiso says. "They will do

anything to make money. Feeding themselves is more important than saving from malaria."

"That makes no sense."

"Their son Demond is a suspect," Kasigo says after a pause.

"What will happen to him?"

"Frankly, nothing, in my opinion."

"How so?"

"That's the way it is here."

Chapter 23

I am busy helping Kasigo. New plans have to be made for the clinic's sessions with the village public. Around four in the afternoon, Kasigo walks over and hands me a note.

"We got a call yesterday when you were not here. So I wrote down the message," she says.

I'm curious. I think it must have been from Rachel. Maybe she is going to visit me, for a change. Instead the message is from Agnes:

Rachel attacked while walking home last evening. She went to talk with Gamba's parents to discuss their son, was harassed, and attacked by two boys looking for money. She's shocked but not injured.

Why did she do that, in spite of warnings? It doesn't matter. I have to go and see her. I tell Kasigo that it is important and urgent for me to leave and not to worry if I am late tomorrow.

I ride my moped as fast as I can. When I reach Rachel's cottage, it is locked. I knock on the door. There's no answer. There is no use asking the kids playing nearby. Frustrated I go over to Agnes's cottage. She's not there either. I rush over to the local

Peace Corps office. They tell me Rachel has already left for the United States. Her problem with the local food and the physical attack was too much for her, and she requested an early release.

I'm back at my cottage, but cannot sleep. I take out my guitar and start humming "Some Day We'll Be Together." I have no idea how long I am up. I sleep without changing my clothes. A week later I make another trip to Blantyre. This time Agnes is there.

"She really wanted to see you before she left," Agnes says. "I'm disappointed that she had to leave in a rush. You can understand what she went through. It's scary to have an incident like that in a foreign country. She was too scared to walk even to her school."

We both keep quiet for a while.

"When did it happen?" I ask.

"About three days before I called you. She sent one of the kids to my cottage asking me to come over. She didn't want you to see her in that condition," she added after a pause.

"Was she injured or something? Any bruises on her body?"

"No. There was nothing visible. But the trauma of the whole thing, you know."

"Yes," I said.

"I'm really sorry. She left this note for you."

The note confirms what Agnes has already told me. Her last words: *I'll really miss you. Thanks for everything.*

I fold the paper and shove it in my pocket. I thank Agnes and return to my village. I was hoping our relationship would become something lasting and joyful in Africa and continue when we returned to America. But that was not in our stars. The only thing left for me is to immerse myself in my duties and complete the remainder of my service.

**Part 3
Demond
1968**

Chapter 24

Akua Ibori got up at five in the morning and woke his son Demond.

"Come on, get going," He said. "Time to start planting."

Demond rubbed his eyes and opened them slightly. It was still dark inside their two-room hut.

The Ibori family lived in a thatched cottage on the outskirts of Zomba. They slept on the floor. At night, Demond covered his face with his hands, so the mosquitoes wouldn't bite the most sensitive part of his body. They were everywhere, especially at night. No one knew how to get rid of them. Sometimes people from the district health department came and sprayed DDT in the air around his house. He could sleep better for a couple of nights, but then the mosquitoes returned again.

Demond heard his mom Bayo grinding corn outside to prepare the *Nsima*. He turned on his side and closed his eyes again. Akua approached him and shook him.

"Get up, I said." Akua's voice raised impatiently.

"Ah. What about school?" Demond asked yawning.

"No school when you have work to do in the farm. What

good is school if you don't have anything to eat?"

Demond pushed up off his sleeping mat and went outside to the common water pump to wash his face and get ready to accompany his father to the field. His younger brother, Badru, and sister Abebi still slept. They were five and three years old—too young to work in the field. Demond was fourteen. He was slim and five feet six inches, tall for his age.

Akua and Demond walked up to the small farm on the outskirts of Zomba, Malawi.

"What we use for the fertilizer Dad, cow manure?" Demond asked.

"Yes. Cow manure," Akua responded as if he was complaining. "You think we are like those rich farmer with lots of money to buy fertilizer."

"Dad, why are we stuck in farming? I'm sure there are other jobs with better pay."

"It's a long story," he said after a pause. "Furthermore it's a family business. I've to keep a promise I made to my dad."

"How so?"

"Well, I was bit older than you, twenty years old to be exact. I married your mom and started helping my dad, your grandpa, in his farm. On the day we found out that your mom was expecting a baby, your grandpa died of a heart attack." Akua wiped his eyes.

"I'm sorry to hear that," Demond said.

"Yes."

"Why didn't you go to school?"

"How could I? I had to help my dad on the field, just like you are doing. Then after he died, I had to learn to be a father and manage the farm that my dad cared so much for."

"But, you have to think of doing something else, Dad. So we don't have to wait six months to eat the corn we are sowing. It's the same story every year."

Akua didn't say anything.

Demond and Akua worked all day, sowing the corn seeds and fertilizing. They came home tired and hungry. This year with Badri and Abebi to look after, Bayo was not able to help Akua. Demond's schooling had to wait.

"We have a good chance to get a good yield this year," Akua said to Bayo as they sat outside their cottage after dinner. "The recent rain should help."

"What do you think we'll do until the harvest?" Bayo asked. "Eat only one meal a day as every year?"

"Yes. We have to manage, just like every year."

Bayo just shook her head in frustration.

Chapter 25

"It's been two months after the planting, Akua," Bayo said to Akua one evening. "We're running out of corn and rice."

"How many times I have to tell you. It'll be another four month or so," Akua said, irritated.

"We're going to die of hunger."

Akua kept quiet.

The supply of corn and rice soon ran out of the Ibori household. With nothing to cook, Bayo sat outside her cottage with her children. Badru and Abebi played in the dirt, came, and hugged her. They caressed Bayo's face with their hands and asked if they could have something to eat. Bayo hugged them tight and cried. Bayo filled a bowl of water and kept it on the fire to pretend that she was cooking. She gave them hot water. Bayo knew the next day would be same.

One day she went to Akua's farm to see if she could salvage some corn even if it was not ready to pull. There she found Akua sitting in a corner and just staring at the plants.

When she came home, she had a surprise waiting. It was her mom, Nomuso, and dad, Macario, sitting on a mat on the floor outside.

"Here, I brought you something," Nomuso said as she put the sack full of rice in front of Bayo.

"Mom, thank you so much. You're a godsend."

"As long as your dad is healthy and keeps his job at the coffee plantation, this much we can do."

Bayo walked inside the cottage with her mom. Nomuso looked around the cottage as if to find where the kids were.

"And how's Dad?" Bayo asked.

"He's okay. But getting old, you know. How long can he bring me here on his bicycle? I don't know. Thinking of him, where's he?"

They went outside. Macario was playing with Abebi and Badru. Demond wasn't around.

Bayo insisted her mom and dad to stay over for dinner, but Nomuso declined.

"We better go before it gets dark," she said and she motioned Macario to leave.

Chapter 26

Demond admired his friend Nanji, who always dressed well and had a carefree manner. They often met on Akua's farm. They huddled in a corner, away from everyone, and smoked cigarettes. Demond had no idea where Nanji got them from.

"Have you ever been hungry?" Demond asked Nanji once.

"Sometimes, and you?"

"Most of the time. This year's been bad."

"What's with the farm your dad has? Doesn't he earn money?"

"Well, we can't sell the corn until it is harvested."

"There's other ways you can make money, you know," Nanji spoke as if he had a secret.

"How?" Demond asked.

"It's easy. Pick pockets. You have to be fast though."

Nanji looked at Demond straight in the eyes and continued, "I'll take you to the big city and show you, if you're interested."

Demond wasn't sure if he wanted to do that. But he saw how his friend was resourceful in getting what he wanted.

Chapter 27

Nomuso's rice didn't last long. The Iboris soon had no food. It would be another month or so before Grandma visited again.

One day Abebi cried all night. She couldn't sleep. Her stomach was growling. Demond was upset. He didn't understand why Akua couldn't find another job or make money so they could eat.

In the morning he left home and walked the streets aimlessly. It was better than listening to Badru and Abebi cry.

By evening he felt weak. Mrs. Kone lived two blocks away from his cottage. Her husband worked on a tobacco farm owned by a rich landlord. He earned good wages. Demond could see a basketful of fruits and vegetables from the street through an open window. He looked around and, not noticing anyone, walked in through the open door. He picked up the basket and ran as fast as he could.

"Where in the world did you get this?" Bayo asked when he reached home.

"I was coming home and saw that Mrs. Kone had these in a basket."

"But you can't just take them without asking."

"Oh, she won't miss it. Besides why should we go hungry? She won't starve. It's just her and Mr. Kone."

"This isn't right."

Bayo said this, but secretly she was glad that she could have some food for her family. She hoped Demond wouldn't get into a habit of stealing. She boiled the bananas for eating that night and saved the rest for the next day.

"Well, don't do that again. They'll catch you and send you to jail," she said as they ate.

Demond didn't respond. But that night everyone slept well.

Next week as Demond was returning home, he saw a stray chicken trotting on the street. He grabbed it and hid under his shirt. He took it to a livestock market and sold it. He came home with money to buy fruit and rice. Bayo didn't ask what he had done.

Demond started accompanying Nanji on his trips into town. Sometimes they worked in pairs, one distracting a tourist and the other picking his pocket. Demond got the hang of it in a few weeks. He didn't tell Bayo or Akua of his escapades, but he brought home money. They didn't question him as long as they had something in their stomach.

"Have you heard about Mrs. Kone?" Bayo asked Akua one evening when they were sitting together for dinner. It was middle of November. The trees had started to turn lush green. Soon it would be time to harvest the corn.

"No," Akua said.

"I heard she has been sick with high fever. For the past few weeks, she has been in coma. Several other people in their neighborhood are sick."

They had heard that people were dying of malaria. Most realized that it was a matter of time before it would affect them. There were not that many doctors nearby, and many couldn't afford to buy medicine. The civic center in the village was always overcrowded.

"She died yesterday," Bayo said as if it was inevitable.

Chapter 28

It was harvest time in January. The yield from Akua's farm was good.

We are lucky. This is going to be a good year for us. Demond you can go back to school, learn to be a teacher or a lawyer and be rich, Akua thought.

At the same time, Bayo started vomiting in the morning. She was tired all the time. Her body had started to change shape, and she knew that it wasn't a case of malaria. She was expecting another child. Akua would have one more mouth to feed.

Bayo visited the village clinic. Kasigo, the nurse, confirmed her pregnancy.

"You need to be careful now that you're with child," Kasigo said. "We'll come by and give you a mosquito net that you should use every night. Also keep the area around your cottage clean and let no water accumulate. That's where the mosquitoes breed."

Bayo listened to all that but wasn't sure how successful she was going to be in implementing the instructions.

Two days later Kasigo visited the Ibori household with a white young man.

"This is Mr. Owen," Kasigo said. "He'll show you how to tie the net around your bed."

Owen did just that. He wished Bayo well with the new baby arriving and all. Bayo was thankful for them coming. She slept well for a week.

"Oh my God," Akua shouted as he entered the hut one evening. "Where's the net? Someone stole the net."

Bayo had been outside and hadn't noticed. Who could it be?

"Demond, Demond," she called.

There was no answer. When Demond returned at night, she asked him if he knew what happened to the net. He smiled but didn't say anything. He simply gave her the money he had earned by selling it.

Bayo gave birth to a baby girl, who didn't survive past two days. She died of complications from multiple infections, the doctors said.

Akua kept his silence. He needed help in picking, storing, shucking the maize. With the help of Demond, he converted the second room of their cottage into a maize storage room.

"We all need to work. This time it is important," Akua said to Bayo. He didn't even ask her about her health after the baby's death and the time in pregnancy.

"I can't help you as much as I used to," Bayo said. "I am

tired."

"Who do you think is going to give us money for your medicine?" Akua was irritated. "Why don't you ask your mom and dad to come and help us?"

"They do what they can, Akua. They are not very rich themselves."

Now that they had maize, Bayo could at least make food for everyone. Akua put even Badri and Abebi to work in shucking the corn.

The grinding, cooking, and preparing of meals were tiring Bayo. She could hardly lift the big pots and pans. Akua was too busy with preparations to market his crop.

One day Bayo didn't get up in the morning. Akua and Demond went to work without breakfast, thinking she was just tired and would get up late. They woke up Badri and Abebi and asked them to start removing the husk from the maize cobs. Demond couldn't concentrate on his work. He had never seen Bayo not work every morning. He returned home and found Bayo still sleeping.

"Mom, Mom, get up." He shook her but there was no reaction.

He ran to get Akua. By the time they had Kasigo to come over, it was too late.

Chapter 29

Namuso and Macario paid for the funeral. Akua was left with managing the children as well as managing his harvest.

With Bayo gone, Akua looked after the children the best way he could. He cooked *Nsima,* but it never was as good as Bayo's. After dinner he and his children sat outside their hut. Akua told them stories of ghosts and goblins that he himself had heard from his father. Demond made excuses to spend time with his friends. In spite of all that happened, Akua was in high spirits with the prospect of making money and maybe sending his children to school.

One morning Badru got up screaming. He was shaking his shirt and jumping as if some devil got into him. Akua approached him to find out what happened. Badru pointed to an insect that he had just brushed away from his shirt. Akua looked at it and his face turned ashen. Badru was pointing at a weevil, a beetle like corn moth. Akua peeked inside the room where he had stored the corn. The weevils were everywhere. He had no idea where they had come from. They had infested the crop. Akua had not used any pesticide to keep the crop safe from these invaders. He also didn't have bins to store the crop. The crop had to be thrown away. What was he going to do now? How were they going to survive the coming months or years?

Chapter 30

Next morning, without telling anyone, Akua woke up when everyone was asleep and just walked away from his home, leaving his family behind. He had mentioned to Demond that there might be other opportunities for him in neighboring towns with large tobacco farms or tea plantations. Demond never imagined that he would go away by himself and leave them behind.

"Damn it, damn it," Demond said aloud when he discovered his father was nowhere around the house. "How can he do this? How can he leave us alone? We are going to die of hunger."

He had no idea how to look after Badru and Abebi.

"Where's Dad?" Badri asked. "Did he go to the farm?"

"I don't know."

"Did he go to get Mommy?"

"Oh, shut up. Just shut up," Demond shouted then spoke more softly. "He has gone to another town to buy stuff. He'll be back soon."

Chapter 31

The day after Akua was gone, Demond walked the ten miles to his grandma's house and told her what had happened.

"I knew it. Your good-for-nothing father never learned how to take care of his farm or his family," Namuso said. She put her hand on his shoulder and consoled him. "Don't worry. We'll figure out a way out of this."

She gathered a sackful of rice and some vegetables. Demond carried one bag on his shoulder, while Namuso carried another. They walked back to Akua's cottage before it got dark.

Demond remembered how, as a child, he had accompanied his mother to the farm. He liked hanging around her when she cooked. Even as a teenager, he snuggled close to her in moments of playfulness. He missed her. With his grandma in the house, he spent most of the time outside—sitting alone somewhere under a tree in his village, dreaming about how he might make money. He didn't want to follow in Akua's footsteps and tend to the farm.

Chapter 32

Demond met his friend Nanji several days a week in areas around his father's farm. He didn't know whether Nanji was an orphan because he never heard him talk about his parents or where he lived. *Maybe they are dead from TB or something*, he thought. Perhaps he lived on the streets. He had told Demond that he worked part time on a tobacco farm.

"Those guys are rich," he said. "They don't pay me well, but at least I have a steady job."

They smoked handmade cigarettes. Demond didn't care where his friend bought the stuff from. Nanji could as well have stolen it from the plantation. One day Nanji offered him a special one wrapped in maize leaves.

"Tell me if you like this one," Nanji said.

"What's this man?" Demond said after one deep puff. He liked the sweet pineapple-like aroma and felt good. He inhaled a second time and started feeling high. A little while later, he felt his eyelids heavy and couldn't keep his eyes open.

"This is *Malawi Gold*. Precious stuff!" He heard Nanji say, but he could hardly hear what he said next.

Demond had never smoked anything like this before. It was a magic potion, an elixir.

"I like it, I like it," Demond said as he closed his eyes.

Nanji nodded. That's the last thing Demond remembered seeing. He was on his back looking at the clear sky and dreaming of a life that would be, if he was rich. He felt like someone had kept a heavy load on his forehead and was preventing him from opening his eyes. As hard as he tried, he couldn't open them. He didn't know how long he dozed off. When he opened his eyes, Nanji was gone.

Chapter 33

Demond didn't know what was to happen to the farm. Now he was the father figure for his two siblings. He would have to learn fast to keep the farm or do something else.

He cleaned up the room where harvested corn was infected with weevils. Every morning he visited the farm but didn't know what to do. There were still some corn stalks in the ground that needed to be pulled and shucked.

When he met Nanji a week later, he told him what had happened.

"What're you going to do?" Nanji asked.

"No idea," Demond replied, staring off in the distance.

"You can't do what your father did. There's not much money in corn. You must do something else," said Nanji, sounding confident.

"Like what?" asked Demond.

"Grow chamba, the *Malawi Gold.*"

"You kidding? How'd I do that?" Demond was suddenly interested.

"I told you I work at the tobacco farm. You think all of it is tobacco? No. Part is a crop of cannabis. You can do the same. Convert part of your farm to a cannabis crop. Your maize crop will be a camouflage."

"I don't know anything about it."

"Believe me. This stuff is very popular with the tourists. You have to be careful, though. There are drug lords, thieves, and the police."

"Is it illegal?"

"Yes."

"Then?"

"Look. There's a lot of potential to make money. The police look the other way, most of the time. They have other important things to do, unless..."

"Unless what?"

"Unless, you flaunt it, openly."

"When can we start?"

"Well. It's too late for this year. This is February, and my people are harvesting this year's crop. We have to wait until August to sow new seeds. If you can somehow survive until then I can help you."

Demond walked back to his hut after Nanji left. Lost in his thoughts, he almost hit a bicyclist coming his way.

"Sorry," he said.

There is some truth to what Nanji says. I must trust him, he thought. *There is risk, but it's worth taking. What else can I do? Badru and Abebi can stay with Grandma, and I will manage it by myself.*

Chapter 34

Six months later...

One week in mid-August, Nanji came with a small bag full of cannabis seeds. Demond didn't ask where he got them and didn't care if Nanji stole them. They found a sunny but secluded spot, behind what remained of the maize stalks, in Demond's farm. They dug a few foot-deep holes and planted the chamba seeds.

"These grow easily," Nanji said. "And multiply."

"What do I have to do?"

"I've seen the people where I work water them regularly. You do the same."

"Seems easy enough."

"And use the cow manure that your dad used for the corn."

Demond nodded.

"How long before we see anything?"

"I've seen full growth in about five to six months. This is August. So we are talking next spring."

"You're the boss," Demond said after a pause.

Chapter 35

Six months later...

The direct sunlight hitting the area had helped the cannabis plants. Demond was standing in front of the bunch of plants he had grown. He put his hand behind a stalk and spread his fingers among the green leaves. He bent and kissed them.

You're my babies. Don't let me down, now, he murmured.

Nanji came that afternoon and helped Demond cut the plants and tie them in small bundles to bring inside his hut.

"We need to dry the stems," Nanji said.

They hung the cannabis stems upside down on rows of string. Demond watched Nanji doing all this, with much curiosity.

A week later the buds were ready to be pulled from the plants. Demond scavenged glass bottles to store the buds. He and Nanji rolled them into cornhusks to make small, smokable joints. The joints didn't look perfect, but it was enough to make a start.

Demond wasn't sure what was going to happen. On one hand, he was looking forward to the adventure, and on the next, he feared possible failure, the inevitable starvation, and death.

Chapter 36

"Let's stay close to home and see how it goes," Nanji suggested.

"Good idea. Have any place in mind?" Demond asked.

"Yes, I do. We have a treasure right in our backyard."

"Which is?"

"The plateau. I have seen a bunch of people there. Sometimes they are alone, other times they come in groups."

"What for?"

"Well, there are streams, tall juniper trees, waterfalls, and inclines where they go hiking, fishing, and horseback riding. It's perfect for us to practice."

"Let's do it."

The young hikers were easy prey. With the money he earned, Demond could afford to install a telephone in his hut and in his grandparents' house.

It had been a month since they started visiting the plateau. Business was slow that day.

"You know," Demond said to Nanji as they were walking along a trail, "it's not good to do business here. Some people know us in the town, and they can get suspicious and report to the authorities."

"Like I told you way back," Nanji said with some authority, "you are okay if you don't flaunt it."

Demond wasn't that sure. One day when he was returning home, the lady next door kept staring at him without saying anything. He wondered if she knew what he was up to. This is a small village, word got around fast.

"This is not good. We should go out of town," he muttered.

Chapter 37

Next week with their backpacks full of their goods, they took the bus to Blantyre. It was only an hour's ride.

"Let me do the talking," Nanji said, and asked Demond to stay close behind and watch.

Blantyre was a much bigger place than Zomba. Easy to get lost and also easy to target many visitors to the many monuments, stores, and the Mandala House. Demond was sure they had made the right decision. He watched as Nanji walked around, nonchalantly, through the crowd at the central market. Nanji stopped at some stalls and talked with the owners, then shook his head and walked on. Demond followed a few steps behind.

"What's happening?" Demond asked when they met in a corner.

"I tried to see if any of them want to sell our stuff, under the table, to their customers."

"And?"

"They don't know us, and they are not sure how good it is."

"What do we do then?"

"Well, I can understand. I left some samples with some of them. Let them try it, and we'll see what happens."

"And if they don't like it, we are doomed."

"Not necessarily. There are always more places to try."

They stopped at a roadside stand and had something to eat. Now they were at a road crossing. Demond saw Nanji break away and approach a person walking toward them. The person looked like a tourist, well dressed with an air of confidence about him.

Demond saw Nanji talk with the man. They were laughing. Nanji took his backpack off his shoulder and reached inside. The next thing Demond saw was the man hit Nanji on the head. He grabbed Nanji by the arms and turned him around as if he was going to handcuff him. Demond couldn't stand by and see the whole thing. He ran and tried to pull the man away from Nanji. The man was strong. He punched Demond so hard that he lost control and fell on his back. He tried to get up, but the man pulled a gun.

"Are you in this together?" the man shouted. Nanji had freed himself and was facing both of them.

"It's okay, man. Maybe we can work something out," Nanji said.

"Are you trying to bribe a law enforcement officer?" The man continued shouting at them.

"No, no, sir."

"Who's your boss? Who are you working with?"

"Nobody. We have no boss." Nanji, the ever confident, seemed a bit shaken.

"Then, where did you get this stuff?"

The man broke a joint and smelled it. He smiled and said, "This is good stuff, really good." He rubbed his palms together and brushed them on his trousers.

He walked a few feet away, turned toward Demond and Nanji, and said loudly, "Don't ever let me catch you again. Now get the hell out of here." The man took both the backpacks as he walked away.

Nanji kept quiet. They'd lost a valuable supply of their income, but it was better than being thrown in jail. How was he supposed to know that he was talking to law enforcement?

"We didn't see his badge," Nanji said when it was all quiet.

"Yes. How do we know he was law enforcement? Maybe he just bluffed."

"Yes, maybe. What's he going to do with all that stuff?"

"I don't know."

Demond and Nanji spent the whole day in Blantyre without any sale. They came back home, empty-handed and depressed.

Chapter 38

Demond had a dream that night. In his dream he was captured by police, thrown in jail, and beaten to reveal his cannabis farm location. Then his farm was burnt to ashes. Demond woke up with a shudder. He was sweating. It was dark inside his hut.

He wanted to talk to someone. He lay on his rattan mat on the floor till morning, then called his grandma, Namuso.

After Akua left, Nomuso had taken Badru and Abebi with her.

"You can't leave them alone all day when you are wandering around town. At least they will have some food every day," she had said.

Demond agreed.

"I'll give you money when I earn some," he had said.

"And how would that be?"

"I'm trying something with my friend."

"God bless you. All I want is for you to be safe. There are plenty of bad people out there."

"I'll be careful." But Demond wasn't sure what he was going to do. All he had was Nanji.

***

Demond was glad he had the telephone link with Namuso.

"Hello, Grandma."

"Hi, Demond. Where've you been?"

"I'm okay. Hanging out with friends. Trying to earn some money."

"You can move in with us, you know. What're you going to do by yourself in that hut?"

"I'll be fine. We need to do something about the farm. How is Badru and Abebi?

"They're fine. A young white man came the other day. He said that he had distributed mosquito nets to you guys. His name? Oben or something."

"Yes. I remember him. He had come with nurse Kosigo. What did he want?"

"He said that he would give free lessons to Badru and Abebi. He also said that he was sorry about what happened to your family and wanted to help."

"That's nice of him."

Demond felt good knowing Badru and Abebi were safe with his grandparents.

Chapter 39

Nanji was busy for a whole week and couldn't meet Demond. Demond spent time futzing around on his farm. That weekend when Nanji came, they discussed their next move.

"I have an idea," Nanji began. "If we go to a place like Lake Malawi, we have a better chance."

"Lake Malawi?"

"Yes. It's a bit far from here, but it's the biggest tourist attraction. It's big."

"How big?"

"I don't know. Miles and miles of sandy beaches. Many hotels and lodges. Would be good for us. We could act like one of the tourists and make new 'friends'; you know what I mean?"

"Worth a try. And we would be away from here, so out of sight and out of suspicion."

"I'm excited."

"I am too."

Chapter 40

The bus trip to Lake Malawi took a couple of days. Demond had never seen sandy beaches stretched so long. The lake was so wide that he couldn't see the other side. Large hotels and private lodges surrounded by plush trees spread around the water. Several tourists were getting ready for snorkeling, scuba diving, fishing, and boating. He looked up at the clear sky and saw a flock of birds migrating southward. The calm of the place and the vastness were enough to make anyone starting a new adventure a bit nervous.

"We can wander around and talk with people without causing suspicion," Nanji said.

"You're right. One can get lost in this place. Who can see us from a distance? But we need to have a plan."

"Here's what we do," said Nanji. "You stay here in one of these hotels. Keep the backpack with you. I'll keep some stuff with me in my pocket. I'll come back for more when I need to. You have a good time and try to see if you can make some contacts with the hotel guests. Be careful. There'll be security and stuff."

"Okay."

Demond hung around a hotel lobby as Nanji scouted the beach. The hotel was like a plantation with a white two-story colonial structure. A large courtyard in the front had palm trees with lounge chairs. A large door in the center took the visitor into a massive lobby. The lobby had leather chairs and a water fountain. A glass jar with water mixed with lemon slices was placed on a table next to the fountain. Demond could see a path to the right that stretched to the back of the building to a swimming pool and more trees. Cool breeze brushed his cheeks.

Demond walked in and sat in one of the chairs. Nobody seemed to mind. There was a man in casual clothes in one corner reading a newspaper. Demond didn't have the courage to approach him. A while later a young couple walked in with suitcases and walked up to the receptionist for check-in. *Perfect customers for me*, Demond thought. Maybe later.

He waited for Nanji to return and brief him. They were to meet after four hours or so.

What's keeping him? Demond spoke to himself when there was no sign of Nanji after what appeared to be more than four hours. He was getting hungry. He walked along the path to the side that led to the back and sat in a chair under an umbrella. A waiter walked up and asked if he wanted anything. He was balancing a small round tray on his right hand. Demond said he was fine and that he was waiting for a friend. The waiter walked away.

Demond sat staring at the ripples in the lake water as the sun reflected off them. When there was no sign of Nanji, he got worried.

"I better see what's happening."

He got up and started walking along the water's edge in the direction Nanji had gone in the morning. A young couple, both wearing large panama hats, walked with shoes in their hands. At a distance, two fishermen were collecting their gear and loading a small boat to go fishing. There was no sign of Nanji. It would have been easy to spot him if he was there, because the beach wasn't crowded.

Demond had no idea where to look for Nanji. He could be anywhere along the shore or could have walked off to a golf course or to one of the other hotels nearby. As he walked he came across a thatched room, probably a bathroom, he thought. Two men came out, smiling. Both wore just shorts and displayed a good tan all over their bodies. Demond walked in hoping to see Nanji inside.

He wasn't there. He looked to his right. There was a rock formation with trees around it. It offered a shaded and secluded spot—perfect for Nanji to conduct their business. As he approached the rock, he thought he heard someone moaning. Walking past the rock, Demond saw a man lying on the ground. He went closer and was shocked to see Nanji.

"What in the world did you do? What happened?" Demond shouted in disbelief, his face turning red.

Nanji's nose was bleeding, and his face was black and blue around his left eye.

"Ah, it hurts," Nanji said, placing his palm on his left eye.

"But what happened? How did you end up here and like this?" Demond squatted next to Nanji and started to examine his face. Nanji brushed his hands away.

Nanji explained that he had approached a friendly looking person, who turned out to be George, an agent for a drug lord from Mozambique. George wanted to know Nanji's source for the cannabis. Nanji didn't want to disclose anything. They got into a fight. George, who was taller and bigger, beat him up and demanded everything he had in his pockets. He gave a stern warning to Nanji that if he saw him again in the area, things could get worse.

Demond helped Nanji to his feet. They walked to the water where Nanji washed his face. They walked back slowly to the same hotel where Demond had been waiting for Nanji.

"Lady Luck is not going to smile on us," Demond said, disgusted. "Wherever we go, they are there."

"It's a tough business, man," Nanji said. "There are a lot of big players. They are making big bucks."

"And they don't want competition."

"Yes."

"What do we do now? We are small fish. We're doomed." Demond touched his forehead with trembling hands.

"We'll think of something," Nanji said. "We have to avoid this place for a while. There are plenty of other places we can go."

"But what's the guarantee George and his friends won't be there?"

"Let's go eat something and think about it," Nanji recommended.

"Aren't people going to ask what happened to you? You look all messed up."

"I'll say I bumped my head against a rock while swimming."

They ate at the bar and had few cold drinks.

"Do you think we are getting roughed up because we look like kids?" Demond asked.

"We don't just look like kids; we are kids."

They didn't have money to rent a room at the hotel and spend the night there, so they walked up to the bus station and slept on the floor. The next day they took the bus back to Zomba, as empty-handed as before.

I'm never going to make money and stay in one of those hotels like those rich bastards, Nanji murmured in the bus. *I'm destined to die hungry.*

Chapter 41

Demond shuddered at the thought of a life without money or food—a fate that guaranteed death.

After the incident in Lake Malawi, Demond and Nanji decided to stay close to home and look for other opportunities.

"Let's try our luck one more time," Nanji said.

"Do we have any choice?" Demond asked.

"Well, let's go to Lilongwe this time. I know that place. It's larger than Blantyre. One never knows."

The Central Craft market in Lilongwe was a fertile ground to meet visitors and also vendors. They spent the whole morning strolling on the grounds, pretending to see the crafts, and trying to make contacts. One vegetable vendor agreed to work with them.

"How's it going to work?" he asked.

Nanji looked around to make sure no one was within earshot, then softly made a deal to split fifty-fifty.

"Be careful," he said. "Best bet is the young white people. The backpackers."

The vendor shook his head and hid the package Nanji gave

him under his cart.

Demond smiled, hoping now they were getting somewhere, but his happiness was short lived. The sky turned gray. It became darker and darker, and it started to rain. The outdoor vendors started to cover their wares.

"Damn it," Nanji cursed.

"What's wrong?"

"Don't look. Walk straight."

"Did you see a ghost?"

"Worse," Nanji whispered. "I think I saw George or someone who looks exactly like him."

"Are you delusional or something? How's that possible?"

The same story again. Demond was disgusted. They kept walking away from the market in the rain. Within a couple of blocks, they saw a sign that said Spice of Life. It was a nondescript Indian restaurant, a single standalone building with a small entry door and windows to each side.

"Let's wait in here until the coast is clear," said Nanji.

Chapter 42

The restaurant was a one-room establishment with twenty tables draped in white tablecloths. Soft Indian instrumental music played in the background. A wall on the left had a framed picture of Lakshmi, the Indian goddess of wealth, draped in a red sari, standing on a lotus flower with two of her four hands pointing down and the other two raised up holding flowers. A wreath of marigold flowers was draped around a dark frame. There was a large, framed photo of the Taj Mahal on the opposite side. Overhead ceiling fans whirled slowly. Demond smelled the aroma of strong spices and fried food. He thought of covering his nose but got used to the smell a while later.

A young man of brown complexion, wearing black trousers and a white shirt tucked in, was standing at the entrance, waiting for the customers. He was of medium height. He smiled softly and welcomed Demond and Nanji.

"Welcome to the Spice of Life. Table for two?" he asked as he picked up two hard-bound, slightly overused menu folders from a table by the door.

Demond and Nanji learned later that his name was Deepak.

"Have you been here before?" Deepak asked in heavily accented English. He handed them paper towels to wipe their wet faces.

"No. No. Not to your restaurant," Nanji replied.

"Hope you like Indian food," he said as Demond and Nanji were seated at a table in the middle of the room.

Demond looked around the room. The restaurant had just started to fill up with the lunchtime crowd. Maybe the rain drove shoppers inside. Being close to the market, it was expected. A policeman wandered in and took a seat two tables away from Demond and Nanji. Demond raised his eyebrows as he looked at Nanji.

"Yes," answered Nanji. "The spicier, the better."

Demond had never eaten anything other than the *Nsima*, but apparently Nanji had. He was ready to experiment. He had no clue about any of the entrees listed on the menu.

Deepak recommended the chicken *biryani* and cucumber *raita* with homemade *naan*. For drinks he recommended the mango *lassi*.

"What are all these dishes?" Demond asked with a puzzled look. "This is all foreign to me."

"Relax," said Nanji. "The *biryani* is rice cooked with chicken and spices, the *raita* is just diced cucumbers mixed in yogurt, the *naan* is round flat bread cooked in an open clay oven, and the *lassi* is just a buttermilk shake."

"Oh," said Demond. "You seem to know a lot about Indian food."

Nanji just smiled.

"So, what do Indians do to get high?" Nanji asked Deepak, very softly, as he took a morsel of chicken *biryani*. Deepak was standing to his right. Demond was afraid he was being too pushy and waited for a response.

Deepak described how only the rich drank liquor in India. It was not a household custom. Then he looked around to make sure that there was nobody nearby, leaned over, and said in a hushed voice, "We have *hashish*."

"What's *hashish*?" asked Demond.

"*Hashish*, you know. *Bhang*," Deepak said, surprised at Demond's ignorance.

Nanji seemed to know and pointed to his backpack.

"Oh. Yes, yes," is all Demond could say.

"It's been used in India for ages," said Deepak. "Even as far back as the time of Emperor Akbar in the fifteenth century, they smoked it in the hookah. Even now some people use it during wedding celebrations. They drink the *bhang lassi*, dance like crazy, and have a great time."

Deepak waved his hands and moved his hips in circular

motion as he said that. Demond and Nanji looked at each other and smiled. Outside the sky had cleared, and the sun was shining. The light from the window reflected on Deepak and created a show of his shadow on the opposite wall like a movie projector. Demond didn't know what a hookah was but guessed it to be some kind of pipe.

"You think you can make a *bhang lassi* for us?" asked Nanji. Demond was surprised at Nanji's straightforward manner. What if Deepak informed the authorities that they were two drug dealers?

Deepak looked at them as if they were joking.

"You mean, here, like, now?" he said in a hushed tone.

"Yes. We can give you the good stuff," Demond said.

Demond discretely showed him a packet he had in his pocket. He was lucky he had his back to the policeman. Before he pulled the packet, he quickly turned and glanced in the direction of the officer. The officer was busy eating and turning the pages of a local newspaper as he ate. As it happened he looked up as if he had some premonition and smiled and waved at Demond. Demond waved back. A truck rolled by on the street outside, and the noise drowned Demond's response. He softly repeated it after it was quiet.

"No, no, no. I'll go to jail," Deepak said as his face reddened, and he looked in the direction of the policeman.

"No need to worry. Look, you make some for us now. You

don't have to tell anyone. You can have some. If you like it, we'll be back. There's plenty where it comes from."

Deepak went inside the kitchen with the sample Demond gave him. He had no idea what to do with it. He took the chef in a corner and explained what was going on. He handed him the packet with strict warning to keep it quiet. The chef didn't have the exact recipe of mixing the cannabis in the lassi, but he was innovative. He concocted an extract by boiling it in water, let it cool, and then mixed with buttermilk, milk, mango pulp, and sugar. He poured the blended concoction in two small glasses and handed them to Deepak.

Deepak smiled and waited a few steps behind their table. He still had that worried look on him as if he had done something terribly wrong. The policeman called him by waving his finger. When Deepak approached him, he extended the fingers of his right hand to make a sign for something tall. Demond and Nanji couldn't hear him, but it appeared he was ordering the *lassi*. A while later the policeman drank his drink and left.

"This tastes great," Demond and Nanji said together, now that the policeman had left. "We'll be back. Maybe your boss wants to sell the *lassi* as a special, unlisted drink. You know, for young tourists looking for a kick." Demond said to Deepak in a hushed tone. He slipped a few more packets of chamba in his hands.

"*Shukria*, thank you," Deepak said with folded hands as he saw them out the door. He had that smile on his face as if he was holding a secret among them.

Demond and Nanji didn't feel anything for the next twenty minutes, only a dry mouth. They were at the bus station, and the next bus was an hour later. They started feeling drowsy in the next half hour. When the bus came, they could barely see the door. They somehow stumbled in and slept all the way to Zomba.

Chapter 43

Demond and Nanji returned to the Spice of Life restaurant after a month. The place was buzzing, and there were no tables available. Four guests were sitting on a bench at the entrance waiting. It was apparent that Deepak had convinced his boss to use the secret ingredient in their *lassi*. The crowd was mostly young backpackers and tourists.

Deepak recognized them coming in. He glanced around to see what he could do to seat them in a secluded spot. There was a metal table close to the kitchen lacking chairs. He brought two folding chairs from inside and motioned them to take their seat. Demond felt like a special guest. The guests waiting at the entrance glanced at them and winced but didn't say anything. The location near the kitchen and the small table wasn't what he liked, but they didn't have to wait, and he was hungry.

"Business is good, huh?" Demond said to Deepak as they were seated.

Deepak nodded with a smile as if they were keeping a mutual secret. He didn't want to say anything or add a commentary.

Demond and Nanji ordered their usual—*chicken* biryani,

naan, and raita. The hot spices burned their tongues, but they liked it. They were busy talking and eating. In hushed tones they discussed ways to increase their cannabis sales and target new customers. Sometimes they used code words, which only they understood. If a person looked amiable and friendly, they called him or her a cat. If a person looked more aggressive, they called him or her a bulldog.

Demond wanted to ask Deepak for a glass of water, but he noticed that he was not around. They had seen him go into the kitchen. Demond wondered if he was upset or just wanted to keep a distance from them.

A young couple in their twenties, he guessed, was sitting two tables down. Both were casually dressed in shorts and sneakers—typical American or European tourists. They were sharing a drink from the same glass with two straws, raising their eyebrows to look at each other like two lovebirds. Demond wanted to walk over and ask them if it was the special *lassi* they were enjoying. He could supply them with the real stuff. Here in the restaurant, it was a bit of a risk. The place was crowded, and any exchange would have been noticed. He remembered the incidents with the police in Blantyre and the encounter with George, who threatened him at Lake Malawi.

Lost in his thoughts, Demond didn't notice Deepak had returned and was standing next to him. He had been gone for more than thirty minutes. He had another man with him. The man wore a dark jacket and white trousers. The jacket looked a size larger and drooped on his shoulders. He had parted his long hair in the middle that left bangs on either side of his eyes. His teeth were stained, perhaps by constant tobacco chewing.

Demond and Nanji exchanged glances not knowing what was happening. Had Deepak called the authorities to hand them over? But they had not done anything openly to raise suspicion.

"Sorry to leave you two alone. Very sorry," Deepak said as he bowed and removed the empty plates. "Is there anything I can bring you?"

Demond requested a glass of water.

"Who do we have here?" Nanji asked.

"Very sorry, again. My boss, Mr. Hari, sir."

Hari was the first one to break the silence before Demond and Nanji opened their mouth.

"How's it going? Looks like you gentleman like Indian food, huh," he said with an accent that sounded like he was elongating each word. He was even shorter than Deepak.

"Yes, sir," Demond said. "And Deepak here has taken good care of us. You should give him a *baksheesh*, a bonus."

"Yes. He's one of our best."

There was a moment of silence when nobody knew what to say.

"You gentlemen care to come by my office in the back when you are done?" Hari asked.

"Sure," Demond and Nanji said together. Demond looked at Nanji with raised eyebrows.

They both skipped the dessert and walked over to Hari's office, wondering what he was up to. Deepak was escorting the people waiting outside to the vacated tables.

Chapter 44

Hari's windowless office was tucked in a corner beside the kitchen. One could hear the rattle of the dishes, the sizzle of the fryer, and occasional chatter in some Indian language, but once the door was closed, it was quiet. The office, if one can call that, was just a bit bigger than a closet. Two overhead florescent tubes emitted dim light and a constant buzz. Hari sat behind a table that had a metal stabber in the right corner on which a stack of receipts was pushed in. There was a thick ledger in the middle of the desk and a dark fountain pen besides it. A calendar with the photo of lord Krishna, hung on the wall facing Hari's desk. In the photo, Krishna had a blue skin with yellow loincloth around his waist. He was standing with his legs crossed and was playing flute as a cow stood behind him. A frame depicting Lord Ganesha, the deity with a human body and elephant's head, hung behind his desk.

These people are really religious, thought Demond.

"We are expanding," Hari said as he motioned to them to sit on two metal chairs facing his desk.

Demond and Nanji nodded, not knowing what was to follow.

"Thank you for helping us grow our business," Hari

continued. "We knew the risk involved, but so far we've been lucky. We've an opportunity to open a branch in the East Village in Lower Manhattan, in New York City."

Hari didn't bow and smile like Deepak. Demond and Nanji looked at him with curiosity. This was getting interesting.

"New York...like...in the United States?" Nanji asked. He beamed, eyes wide open.

"Yes, sir. It'll be a simple restaurant with an added feature. A hookah bar in the back," Hari said with an animated gesture. He said his brother Ranjan, who lived in New York's Lower East Side, talked about the hippies with long hair, who showed a free spirit and looked for a cool place to hang out, listen to soothing music, and get high to forget the stress of the war thousands of miles away. He said these youngsters were protesting the war in Vietnam and were looking for an outlet for their frustrations against the government's actions in the war, the death of innocent lives.

"Your stuff will be very popular with the sitar music in the background," Hari added. "Can you provide it in larger quantities?"

"Sure. We'll do all we can to meet your needs," Demond said when Hari stopped talking. "Just give us advance notice."

"Of course."

"I'll call you in a few days," Hari said.

Demond and Nanji shook hands with Hari and left the restaurant. Once out on the street, they gave each other a high five. Demond shouted, "Yahoo!" and did a few dance steps on the street.

They had finally seen the light at the end of the tunnel, maybe. They had made a commitment but had no idea whether they could honor it in good faith. It might involve buying more land for farming and employing more people. In addition to increasing the quantity of the crop, there was the logistics of packaging and exporting the stuff abroad. Perhaps Demond's brother Badri could help.

With whatever money Demond was making, he could have moved to a better place with his brother and sister. But he had decided against it. It was better not to show off too much to avoid causing suspicion. He thought perhaps, if everything works out, he would be able to fulfill his dream by going to America. But there was no guarantee that Hari would keep his word. What if he only raised their hopes and then backed off?

Chapter 45

A couple of months passed by, and there was no news from Hari. Demond had left his telephone number with him. He thought he would call Hari if nothing happened for another month.

The phone rang as Demond was leaving for a short trip to Blantyre. Demond smiled as he took the receiver in his hands.

"Hello, Mr. Demond," he heard someone say.

It was Hari.

"Good to hear from you. I was wondering—" Demond started but was cut short.

"I'd like you to come again to our restaurant, Mr. Demond. We need to talk more about our scheme. We can't do it over phone, you know."

"Yes, I understand. When do you want us to come by?"

"At your convenience. In a week or so?"

"Sure. That'd be great!"

Chapter 46

When Demond and Nanji visited Spice of Life, Hari was waiting for them.

"To my office, please. Are you hungry? Should I get you something? It'll be on the house."

Demond and Nanji said they were fine. Hari took them to his office. He stepped out for a while and came in and sat in his chair facing them. Deepak appeared with a plate of samosas and two cups of tea. He knowingly smiled at them.

"Well, things are coming together, sooner than I expected," Hari started. "My brother Ranjan has signed a lease for the restaurant. He will arrange for one of you to get a passport and US visa with work permit for a skilled chef for the restaurant."

Demond and Nanji had to decide which one it was going to be. Hari also promised to pay for the person's passage to New York. Whoever decided to go to New York would smuggle the cannabis buried in packages of spices.

"If you're careful, things will work out. Please remember that if you get in trouble, I won't have anything to do with it."

"Understood and agreed!" Demond and Nanji said simultaneously.

Chapter 47

On their way back, Nanji said he wasn't interested in leaving Malawi. He already had a job and was just helping Demond start a new business. They decided that Nanji would manage the farm and Badri and Abebi would stay with the grandparents. Nanji would reduce the maize crop and instead plant more cannabis. Macario would help when he retired from his job.

When alone in his hut, Demond broke out in a hysterical laughter. He didn't want to tell this to anyone, yet. He was superstitious that way. If things worked out like he was hoping, there was going to be better life for everyone. He didn't have any hope that he would see his father again. At least he was doing better than his father in taking care of the family. No one was going to be hungry anymore.

Demond had no idea what lay in his future, but for the first time, he felt the gods were smiling upon him.

Part 4
Thirty Years Later
2000

Ashok Shenolikar

Chapter 48

The guests started arriving at six thirty in the evening. It was mid-August and still bright and sunny.

Today's party was to celebrate Owen being included in Long Island's Fifty Best Doctors for the year 2000. For weeks Agnes had been over the moon with excitement. She made sure that all the prominent physicians on Long Island were invited. There would be a cocktail hour followed by a buffet dinner.

She had a blow up of Owen's picture from *Newsday*, framed and placed it on an easel near the swimming pool. It showed Owen wearing a striped burgundy tie, a light-blue shirt, and the white lab coat. Agnes had selected the tie herself. In all the years they'd been married, she'd never been so proud. She knew Owen hated surprises so hadn't tried to make it a surprise party. That would not go over well at all.

Sally walked in as she was checking the menu one last time.

"Hi, Mom. Today's a special day for you guys."

"That's right."

"And this November is your twentieth wedding

anniversary. It's turning into quite a big year." Sally shook her head, smiling. "You never told me how you two met, except that you were both in the Peace Corps."

"Well. Yes and no."

"What does that mean?"

"Your dad was in the Peace Corps. I was with USAID. He used to visit my friend Rachel, who lived close by. She left her assignment early because of her health and other matters. I lost touch with her and your dad after that."

"Then?"

"It's a long story. Someday I'll tell you. Right now we better make sure we have everything in order."

"What do you want me to do?"

"Make sure all the tables and chairs are set up in the backyard. And oh, bring the boom box from upstairs and set it in the back, away from the pool so it will be kind of hidden."

After Sally left Agnes stared out the window. Back in 1980, she had been visiting her friend Jody in Huntington. Jody had to take her son to see a pediatrician. Agnes accompanied her and was surprised to discover that the doctor was Owen. It was bit awkward to run into him after over a decade. But Owen had seemed happy to see her again. A whirlwind romance followed.

Oh well, I'm glad it turned out the way it did, she said to herself and called the caterer to make sure they were going to arrive in time.

"Make sure you come home early, honey," Agnes had warned Owen as he left for his office that morning. She hoped that he wouldn't forget, as he usually did when he got busy with a patient.

Owen cancelled his last appointment. It was a well-baby appointment that could be postponed for the next day. A pharmaceutical company had sent a calendar with a picture of a tropical location for each month. The current month's pick, Kenya, made him think of his days in the Peace Corps in Malawi in the late '60s, almost forty years ago. He was a young man then, unsure of his future but wanting to be of help to people.

On his way home, he felt a throbbing pain in his back that moved down his spine. *There it is again*, he thought. The pain was acute at times, refusing to go away with over-the-counter pills. He had seen his friend Dr. Trivedi, a neurologist, at the Stony Brook hospital. After an MRI and other tests, Dr. Trivedi had concluded that Owen might be suffering from a nervous system disorder, which if it persisted could require surgery. Owen was not in favor of undergoing surgery, if the problem could be resolved by other nonintrusive means. He dreaded the thought of being confined to a wheelchair, forced to close his practice. He hoped it wouldn't come to that. Several medical journals claimed that marijuana helped relieve chronic pain, in at least some patients. But it was a banned substance.

Should I try it? But where would I get it here on Long

Island? I don't want to roam the streets of Manhattan, incognito and, God forbid, get caught by the police.

He took a hot shower and changed into casual clothes—brown Dockers, a long-sleeve sports shirt from J. Crew that he particularly liked, and penny loafers. He looked down on the backyard from the upstairs bathroom window. All the festive decorations were in place. Sally was making rounds, checking things. Agnes looked beautiful in her new blue dress with a short pearl necklace he had given her on Christmas the year before. He remembered their encounter in his office, their romance, and the wedding. He smiled. He was having a good life, so far, but for the chronic pain in his back.

He came downstairs a few minutes before six thirty to welcome their guests. Ten minutes into the party, he noticed a familiar face.

"Owen, my good friend, congratulations!" Andy approached him with an extended hand.

His classmate from the medical school had become a psychiatrist. They reminisced about their college days.

"How do you manage to keep yourself so fit?" Andy said.

"It's not magic. I still run every morning and watch what I eat. But lately I'm having issues with my back." Owen rotated his shoulders to relieve the stress tugging at his back muscles.

"Ah, don't worry. You're still a young man. It'll go away." Andy patted Owen on his shoulder as he walked over to meet someone else he recognized.

Owen himself thought so. The pain didn't prevent him from his morning runs, for which he was grateful.

By seven thirty the party was in full swing. All the invited guests had arrived. Agnes was moving around, making sure everyone was enjoying themselves and accepting congratulatory greetings and comments about how great the party was and for all her efforts in arranging it. She had put light music on the cassette player with songs from the '70s—Peter, Paul and Mary; James Taylor; Marvin Gaye; and others of her favorites. The speakers placed near the swimming pool spread the music around the backyard. Some songs reminded Owen of his days during the Vietnam War.

"Owen, I'd like you to meet Dr. Rodriguez."

Owen's younger sister, Dana, was standing in front of him with a young man who appeared to be in his late thirties or early forties. He was dressed in business casual, sporting long black hair that curled over his neck.

Owen greeted him with a handshake.

"First, my hearty congratulations to you, Dr. Martin," Rodriguez said. "It's my privilege to meet such a famous person."

"Thank you. You can call me Owen. It's not a big deal really."

"Yes, it is. You are too humble. You must have plenty of

satisfied patients, and your colleagues obviously admire you."

"Is that how it works?"

"Yes, as far as I know."

"What brings you to Long Island? And how do you know Dana?"

"I'm a chiropractor practicing in Manhattan, but I've been Dana and Roger's neighbor for a long time. I took a day off to attend the Chiropractic Supplies Tradeshow at the Nassau Coliseum. They always have new devices on display."

Dana left them and moved on to talk with other guests.

"Tell me, Dr. Rodriguez, do they have any device to alleviate chronic back pain?" Owen asked. He hadn't seen any advertised in the medical journals he read, but he asked Rodriguez to keep the conversation going.

"What kind of back pain? And call me Juan."

"Juan, then. I'm a children's doctor, not a specialist in neurology or orthopedics. But my good friend Trivedi tells me that I may have a nervous disorder."

"*The* Dr. Trivedi from Stony Brook? He's the best."

"I know, but he says I may need surgery, which I don't like, if I can help it."

"I can recommend something, but you may not like this either."

"And what would that be?"

"Cannabis." Juan whispered as he looked around to make sure nobody was listening, and then said a little louder, "Because of the nature of my practice, I did a lot of reading on it. Unfortunately, it's still a federal offense to buy cannabis."

"I know." Owen felt disappointed that he'd learned nothing new.

"You can buy the stuff on the streets in East Village in Lower Manhattan on any Saturday. I don't know how they do it."

"I don't want to risk that."

"I don't blame you. Let me think. When I was in college, there was a bar on Lower East Side that had a hookah bar. I don't know if they are still open."

Juan took out his iPhone and swiped the screen a few times.

"Yes. They are still open," he said with a wide smile. "Do you smoke a pipe?"

"Occasionally!"

"Then you're in business. Just use that stuff instead of the tobacco. It will smell though."

Owen thanked him and said he would look into it.

"Let me know if I can be of any help," Juan said as he moved away to mingle with other guests.

The party was over by eleven o'clock that night. Agnes and Owen personally thanked all guests for coming and walked them out. The weather was getting a bit nippy with a mild breeze. Some close friends lingered on. Agnes ordered the waiters to bring fresh coffee.

When they were alone together in bed that night, Owen mentioned his conversation with Juan.

"It's risky but worth a try," Owen said.

Agnes yawned, her eyes half closed and looking down at his right wrist. Owen realized he was rubbing it with his other hand. His hand was trembling.

"Owen, are you okay?" she asked. "Your hand is shaking. Is this something new? Did you have too much to drink?"

"Go to sleep." Owen sighed. "We had a long day." She kissed him lightly, said okay, and the next minute, she was snoring.

Owen gazed down at her. She looked so happy. He didn't want her to worry about his condition. There had been times when, during his examination of a patient, his hands had begun to tremble. None of his patients or their parents had noticed it.

He stayed awake for a while, disturbed by the thought of doing something illegal. The tremor in his hand had quieted down. He got up, walked down to his study, and turned on the computer where he kept his diary.

It was good I ran into Juan. He confirmed what I already knew about the benefits of cannabis. I always thought it was only for junkies. But the journals are saying it is potent and can be used for medical purposes to relieve pain, especially chronic pain.

His reputation was at stake. All those things he had worked so hard to achieve, culminating in being selected as one of the fifty best doctors on Long Island, would be gone in a second of indiscretion. At the same time, he didn't want to suffer in vain when something could be done discreetly.

After completing his entry, he turned off the computer, sat in his chair in quiet concentration, then got up and went upstairs to sleep.

Chapter 49

On a cold Saturday afternoon, a month after the party, Owen's brother-in-law, Roger, knocked on his door. He had come to pick him up as promised. They were on their way to Manhattan to visit the hookah bar.

It had been years since Owen had set foot in New York City. As newlyweds, he and Agnes frequented Rockefeller Center during the Christmas season. They walked hand in hand along Fifth Avenue, sometimes stopping by Saks to look at bottles of eighty-dollar perfume. It was all magical. The birth of Sally and his growing pediatric practice put a damper on their visits to the city. They preferred to spend time locally.

The traffic on the Long Island Expressway was bad as usual, especially as they approached the midtown tunnel, with multiple lanes merging into two. Owen wondered how people commuted to the city every day. He could see the top of the Empire State Building, all lit up with red and green colors from projected lights. When they entered the city, Owen understood why people commuted to the city. Manhattan was an alternate universe. The hustle and bustle on the streets sandwiched between tall buildings contrasted with the tranquil treelined suburbs. Yellow taxies whizzed by, and cars of all makes and models drove alongside them as sirens of fire trucks wailed in the distance. Garbage trucks waited parallel to the parked cars, collecting garbage even at this late hour. Pedestrians crossed the streets as the signals changed to green, leaving no time for the waiting cars to make a turn. Owen was glad he was not driving.

Rodriguez had only said that the restaurant's name was Spice of Life and it was somewhere on A Avenue on the Lower East Side. *You won't miss it if you walk east on Fourteenth Street and make a right on A Avenue,* were his exact words. Roger made the first left turn on Second Avenue and drove south. That part of Manhattan was not crowded. Approaching Fifteenth Street he saw a sign for a parking garage. There was no room to park on the street with cars already packed end-to-end, almost touching each other. It was a miracle how those who parked there had done so with such perfection, leaving only an inch or so between each car. Owen wondered how they would ever manage to get out.

"I don't even remember parallel parking, do you?" Owen asked Roger.

"No," Roger said and added, "Even if I did I don't want to risk it here. In this neighborhood, I'm not sure if the car will be there when we return, or if it is, it might have been vandalized."

They found a parking garage on Fifteenth Street. After getting the stub, they turned right out of the garage and started walking. They just needed to walk a couple of blocks, find A Avenue, and that would be it. It took them fifteen minutes to realize that they were heading west instead of east. They asked a cop at a cross street, and he directed them to go down a block and make a left. So, they walked and walked. *Where is this Avenue A? Why is it so difficult to find?* They saw an amiable Asian man walking with his youngish girlfriend.

"You came too far," he said. "This is Chinatown. Go up this way." He pointed.

Owen felt like giving up but wasn't sure how to reach the Fifteenth Street from where they were. They had the parking stub with their address. Maybe they could take a cab.

"Let's keep walking a bit," Owen said, and they did.

It was getting dark, and they didn't want to look like tourists staring at each storefront to read the name. Twenty minutes later, they found a nondescript restaurant tucked between a Bagel Buddy and an Ace Hardware store. The name over the entrance was faded and a red-and-white sign read, Spice of Life. It wasn't hard to figure out that this was the place they had been looking for. They could see, through the parted red curtains, waiters serving the patrons in dim light.

The Spice of Life was still in business.

"Table for two, sir?" A middle-aged man with a slight paunch approached them with two black menus with worn corners. The restaurant was small and quiet.

All the walking had made Owen thirsty and hungry.

"Yes, please," Roger said.

Fortunately, they were seated in the back. They ordered some samosas and a cold drink. There was no sign of a hookah bar. Was this the correct place? Owen didn't know how to inquire. When the waiter approached to ask if there would be anything else, Roger spoke in a hushed tone.

"Where's your bar?" he asked, hoping the man would get his drift.

"Would you like a beer or a drink from the bar, sir?"

"No, no. The hookah bar. Where is it?"

The waiter looked uneasy, as if he might be worried that they were police.

"Don't worry," Owen reassured him. "A friend recommended us to your place."

"Wait a minute, sir."

The manager returned with a tall, thin black man who smiled at Owen.

"Demond, please take these gentlemen upstairs," he said.

"Follow me please," Demond said.

They walked past the kitchen to a narrow wooden staircase to the left. The boards creaked at every step. A small foyer at the top led to a green door to the right and a restroom to the left. Owen smelled a sweet, fruity aroma. As Demond opened the green door, a whiff of smoke trickled out. The room was a small rectangle, smoke-filled, and dark. A few patrons sat on the floor on thin mattresses, some reclining against long round bolster pillows. Soft Indian instrumental music played in the background. Four brass metal pots with narrow necks and fat bottoms, each with a long pipe attached on one side, stood in the middle of the room.

"Take a seat anywhere, sir," Demond said, and asked if it was their first time there.

"Yes," Owen answered.

Demond described that they had a choice of tobaccos in various flavors—apple, cherry, vanilla, and many more. Owen said softly that he was interested in trying weed. Demond nodded and told them he'd be right back. Soon, he returned with a pouch, but as he came closer, he stared into Owen's face from up close.

"Pardon me, but you look very familiar. Have we met somewhere before?"

Owen shrugged. "Let's see. Where would that be? Have you visited my office? But it's in Huntington, Long Island, and I treat children."

"No, no. I think it must have been before I came to America. In another country." Demond scratched his head trying to remember.

"The only time I was outside of America was when I was drafted and in Vietnam." But then he added, "Oh and then as a Peace Corps volunteer in Malawi."

Demond touched his temples with the fingers of his right hand, as if he'd had an instant flash of memory.

"Well, of course. Could it be? Could it be you are Mr. Oben?"

"Oben? No. I'm Dr. Owen Martin."

"Dr. Martin. I'm Demond. You remember? You taught my brother English and mathematics."

"Oh my." Owen smiled. "It's been so long, and you have changed. You are taller. What are you doing here?"

Owen remembered Demond, who had stolen the mosquito nets from his family. He had been furious at the time. He wondered what could have brought the young man to America.

Demond told Owen that now he was a US citizen and was married. He looked as if there was something more he was considering telling Owen about his past, but he quickly said, "Let me know if I can be of any help, Dr. Owen." And he turned to go back downstairs.

Owen didn't want to spend too much time in the hookah bar. After forty-five minutes, he'd gotten an idea what smoking the marijuana felt like then he told Roger he wanted to leave. Roger hadn't smoked because he was afraid of getting high and wouldn't be able to drive back to Long Island.

Demond saw them coming down and took Owen aside. He handed him a neatly wrapped pouch.

"This is on the house. My gift to you. Call me if you need more." And he handed him his card.

Chapter 50

When Owen saw Mrs. Tipton's name on the list that morning, he smiled and placed a check mark against it. He had started his practice twenty five years ago. In those days, the parents of his patients used to believe in the knowledge possessed by the doctors. When the doctor diagnosed an ailment and prescribed a medicine, it was taken as a gospel. But lately things had changed.

People like Mrs. Tipton were educated professionals and computer savvy. They parsed the Internet and mined the data for symptoms before they came in to see their doctor. Mrs. Tipton, for example, would quote WebMD or what she had heard on TV from Dr. Oz or Sanjay Gupta.

"What can I do for you today, Mrs. Tipton?" Owen asked as she entered his office with her son, Aaron.

The boy's mother seemed very worried. "Doctor, I'm afraid Aaron has an internal injury to his knee." She pointed to Aaron's knee.

Owen always kept his cool and tried to convince his patient's parents that their child's case was different from what they had read about. To be a good doctor, he knew he had to be patient. *Just as in shopping where the customer is always right, in medical practice, the patient is always right*, thought Owen—even though sometimes misguided. If a doctor acted angry or argumentative, he soon acquired a bad reputation and started losing patients.

"How are you, Aaron?" Owen said, turning to the child. "How's your football practice?"

"I haven't played since last week. I can't walk," Aaron said, with a sad face.

"Would you like to tell me when this started hurting and how it happened?"

"Doctor, do you think he tore his ACL?" Mrs. Tipton interjected without waiting for her son to speak. She looked very serious.

"Why don't you tell me what happened, Aaron?" Owen again asked the young boy, ignoring his mother.

"I was running on the field, sort of warming up. All of a sudden, I get this pain in my knee, like something moved."

"Let's see." Owen asked Aaron to stand on one leg, the one with the bum knee.

Aaron had difficulty putting his weight on the leg. Owen asked Aaron to lie down on his back on the examination table. He bent his knees and pressed the muscles behind his thigh and asked where it hurt. Aaron made an "ouch" sound when Owen pressed his thigh.

"Could it be sciatica?" It was Mrs. Tipton again.

Owen wanted to ignore her but resisted. It was better to be patient and explain.

"I'm glad you are considering the possibilities, Mrs. Tipton, but I think Aaron is lucky. He seems to have pulled his hamstring. It happens and happens suddenly," Owen said calmly.

"But why would he feel pain in his knee?"

"Mom!" Aaron glared at his mother, clearly embarrassed by her interruptions.

"Okay. Okay. But I read about all these symptoms on WebMD. I was worried."

"That's okay, Mrs. Tipton," Owen said. "It's good to do research, but one can't trust everything on the Internet. They only give generic information and a myriad of possibilities. Only a personal exam in a doctor's office confirms a diagnosis."

Mrs. Tipton looked deflated and quieted down.

"Here's what I am going to recommend," Owen said, turning toward Aaron. "I'll print out some exercises for you to do. Follow the instructions. It will take a few weeks, but I bet you'll be back to normal before you know it."

"Thanks, Doc."

"If there is a problem, or if you have any more questions, just send me an e-mail." Owen escorted them out.

"Do we need a follow-up appointment?"

"We'll wait and see, Mrs. Tipton. Keep me informed on Aaron's progress."

Owen knew that wasn't the end of it. He had an idea.

Owen wanted to make the best use of the technology. He hired a web-design service that created a website for his practice. The website displayed information about common health problems and helpful hints for how to cope with them. It also had a feature where his patients could send him a message for follow-up and receive an answer without coming into the office. As an active member of the American Association of Pediatrics (AAP), he attended their annual conferences and seminars to increase his professional network and to keep on top of the latest technology, procedures, and instruments. In his diary he collected special cases and encounters with his patients.

One day in November, Owen was pleasantly surprised to receive a letter from the AAP at his office address. He knew he was current with his dues for the year. Perhaps it was an advance notice of the next year's conference. He was partially right. The letter did mention that the 2001 conference was to be held in Montego Bay, Jamaica. He read on:

The AAP 2001 conference committee is in the process of finalizing its program. We would like to invite you to be a member of a panel to discuss the effect of the Internet on patient behavior. Your experience and insight would be of immense value to the membership.

Owen was planning to attend the conference as he did every year, but the surprise invitation to participate in a panel discussion was more of a reason to do so. He took a deep breath after reading the invitation. He was proud that he had been selected to take part in a panel. It was an honor and a professional recognition by his peers. He put the letter in his coat pocket lest he forget later on. He wanted Agnes to see it for herself.

Upon returning home that night, he showed the letter to Agnes and asked her if she would like to accompany him. She had never been to the Caribbean and readily agreed. She started thinking of things she could do while Owen was busy with his meetings. There was the town of Negril she could visit for shopping. She was sure the conference committee would arrange for an excursion. She was charged up and began planning to shop for clothes she should have for the trip. Although her wardrobe was substantial, Agnes always bought something new for special occasions.

Before the last date for a response, Owen sent a letter to the conference committee: *It will be an honor to be part of this distinguished panel.*

From then on, at every opportunity, Owen kept copious notes about his interactions with patients who showed Internet knowledge and demonstrated so in their communications with him. He was still concerned with facing an audience and making a good impression, but at least he would go well prepared.

Chapter 51

In April 2001, Owen left for Montego Bay accompanied by Agnes. Their daughter, Sally, was now married and living in Commack, only ten miles from Huntington. They said they would call her and let her know how Owen's appearance in the panel was received by the audience.

Owen was busy with the conference proceedings. Every day there was a new keynote speaker. Each one was a famous doctor from the United States or from other places as far away as Tokyo, Japan. They regaled the audience with humorous stories about their patients' behavior and how they dealt with difficult situations. Owen wondered if he would be just as good in front of people he had never met before. The exhibition hall was full of representatives from pharmaceutical companies demonstrating new medications.

"I'm glad I came to this conference," Owen said to Agnes over dinner the second day. "I hope I won't make a fool of myself tomorrow."

"Relax. You'll do all right," Agnes said. "Have another glass of wine and get a good night's sleep."

His panel discussion would be at one o'clock the next day.

In the morning, he sauntered over to the hall where it was going to be. He wanted to get an idea of the surroundings, the stage where he would be sitting, and the size of the room. He peeked into the hall. A session was in progress. The coordinator was sitting on the dais, and the speakers were standing at the level of the audience. They probably liked being close to the audience. Some of them would walk forward to answer a question as if they wanted to meet the person. Owen imagined himself on the dais and felt more comfortable. He preferred to keep a distance from the audience.

The panel moderator for his session was an editor from the *American Journal of Pediatrics*. He looked very young and walked and talked confidently. He wore light-blue, faded jeans, a white shirt, blue blazer, and no tie. Every once in a while he moved his fingers through his long hair as he turned his face upward. *It's a new generation*, Owen thought. He, on the other hand, wore his best blue suit, a white shirt, and a greenish tie with yellow polka dots.

There were four panelists. In addition to Owen, there were Dr. Blumenthal from California, Dr. Khaitan from Ohio, and Dr. Sheldon from Texas. Each had to make a five-minute opening statement, and then the moderator opened the floor to questions from the audience. Questions ranged from the validity of the information available to the patients to the various online sources, the psychology of informed patients, and their attitude toward their doctors. By the time it was over, Owen was surprised to realize they had been talking for three hours, and the audience wanted to ask still more questions. One of the questions addressed to Owen was whether he had lost any patients because of his inability to answer questions from an Internet-savvy parent?

"No, I can't say I have," replied Owen. "On the other hand, I have seen an increase in new patients—probably because of word of mouth. Some have even told me that they were very happy and impressed by my website and how it has helped them get more information and contact me easily."

There was a loud applause from the audience. Owen smiled in acknowledgment. He said thank you, but he doubted if they heard him.

"We have time for just a couple of questions," said the moderator turning to the audience.

A man got up from the middle of the room and raised his hand. He wore a wrinkled sports jacket and had disheveled hair. With his unshaven face, he could have passed for one of the homeless people on a street corner asking if you can spare a dollar.

"I've a question for the doctor in blue," he said.

Owen was the only one wearing a blue suit. He got up and walked to the front of the podium.

"You talked of the Internet," the man shouted. "What about the pharmaceutical conglomerate? How much do they pay you to write those expensive prescriptions? How much do they pay you to buy those expensive suits?"

Owen tried hard to stay calm. He started to say something,

but the man started rattling off another question. The conference security had to intervene and take him away.

Owen was a bit rattled by the unexpected intrusion. He was glad there was nothing he could not answer during the formal session. He had cited real-life experiences with his patients without revealing their identities. But after the incident with the rude attendee, he struggled to keep his cool. He wiped the perspiration off his face. This was the first time someone had questioned his integrity.

Chapter 52

On their way back to New York, Owen decided to dress down in shorts, a sports shirt, and sneakers. He wore his *OU* baseball cap. *No one will recognize me now*, he thought. Agnes wore a floral dress. He had told her about the rude interruption, but she didn't say anything.

They had nothing to do at the hotel. They arrived at the airport early for window-shopping and to buy souvenirs for Sally. As they passed a jewelry store, Owen noticed a middle-aged couple. The man was wearing Dockers and a sports jacket. He seemed to be staring at Owen as if he wanted to ask him something. When Owen and Agnes finished their purchase, they started to return to the gate. Owen noticed that the couple was waiting for them. Owen wondered what was going on.

"Are you folks from Oklahoma?" the man asked.

"Oh, yes, of course," replied Owen. "Norman, Oklahoma. I was student at the university there. But now I live in Huntington, New York. I'm a practicing pediatrician there. I am Owen."

"Hi, I'm Ash," the man said.

Ash introduced his wife, Samantha, and said that he too was an alumnus of the university and had lived on Asp Avenue at one time. He asked Owen if he remembered Rickner's bookstore just off the main campus.

Owen said he did.

"How about the McDonald's that sold fifteen-cent hamburgers?" the man asked.

"Yes! On Jenkins," Owen said.

Owen started to feel some familiarity with the man but couldn't figure out why.

"Maybe we were in some classes together," Owen said.

They could have continued talking, but there was an announcement on the airport speaker system. Owen thought it was the boarding call for their flight.

"Go Sooners!" said Agnes with thumbs up as they turned away from the couple. She had been quiet all along but was intently listening to the conversation.

"God bless!" Owen said as they departed.

"Owen, Owen!" the man suddenly shouted as he dashed forward, followed by his wife.

Owen looked around from where he'd stopped in front of their gate to check the flight monitor.

"Excuse me. Are you the Owen who lived on Lindsay Street and owned a Renault?" Ash asked, sounding out of breath.

Puzzled, Owen admitted that he in fact was the same

Owen. Then the man reintroduced himself as Ashley Wilkins.

"Ashley? The quiet one?" Owen beamed as he hugged his old friend from college.

"Sorry for not recognizing you," Ashley apologized.

"Well, we have changed, haven't we?" Owen said. "I thought you looked familiar."

"I wouldn't have noticed you if you weren't wearing your cap," Ashley said.

It turned out the announcement Owen heard was for another flight and they had another half hour, as did Ashley. The four of them walked over to a coffee shop to catch up.

Owen told them that after he finished his work in Africa, he returned to the United States. He didn't mention what happened to Rachel. In New York he enrolled in medical school and later became a pediatrician. He married Agnes, and they had one daughter, Sally, a teacher in Commack. Both of his parents had passed away. Ashley told him about the life of a faculty member at Michigan State, and his three children—two of them professionals and one still in college—the campus politics, the pressure to publish, and the struggle to get tenure. He said they were in Jamaica on vacation.

They had a good chat. At the end, they exchanged addresses and telephone numbers. Ashley invited Owen and Agnes to spend Thanksgiving with them.

"It's a date," Owen said as they departed.

Chapter 53

On a bright, clear day in early October, Owen sprinted out of his house at seven o'clock in the morning. He had donned his Under Armour shorts, T-shirt, and Brooks Adrenaline sneakers— attire fit for a serious runner. He did his regular prerun warm up— a few lunges, bending each knee, and grabbing the foot one at a time by the ankle, before he crossed the street to run on a sidewalk in the opposite direction of the traffic. A full day lay ahead of him with four new patients to see. New patients meant more time spent in getting their history of prior ailments and family background.

The visit to Michigan to meet his longtime friend Ashley for Thanksgiving was also on his mind. He was feeling good after he had started smoking the cannabis Demond had given to him. His pain much relieved. He had called Demond for a fresh supply.

A block away, a garbage truck was collecting trash. As the truck came down the street, he could hear the thumps of the mechanical arm as it periodically stopped in front of a house and unloaded the trash in a collector, disturbing the otherwise quiet neighborhood. An elderly Indian couple walked slowly with hands intertwined, as if to support each other. He waved at them, and they reciprocated with a smile. Two houses down, workers from a lawn service company were taking the equipment out of their truck. The truck was blocking the driveway, and he had to run around it.

A mile further down the street, at a T-intersection, he stopped and looked both ways for approaching cars, then crossed the street and turned left, following his normal route. Owen waved to his neighbor Ted, who was walking his dog Dusti, a German shepherd. Ted was talking to someone on his phone. Owen had picked up his speed and was fifty feet ahead of Ted when he felt a gust of wind, as if something had just whizzed past to his left. It wasn't another person, or a bicyclist but a brown object. He turned and saw that Dusti had gotten away from Ted—his leash dangling behind him. The dog chased a squirrel that ran across to the opposite side of the street. Owen, always ready to help his friends, ran after the dog. Dusti disappeared into bushes behind a brick colonial house.

Ted increased his pace. As he crossed the street, a car swerved past him toward Owen then sped away. Ted heard a noise like a boxer hitting a punching bag. When he reached the colonial house and swept the bushes away, he noticed Owen flat on his back on the lawn, unconscious—Dusti standing at the far end of the lawn, staring up a tree with his tongue out. There were no visible signs of scratches or bleeding, but Owen wasn't moving. Ted called 911 from his cell, and then he called Agnes.

"What?" Agnes shouted. "Where? What happened?"

Ted told her where he was. "He could be badly hurt; I can't

tell. I think you should come immediately."

Three police cruisers arrived within minutes with blaring horns and flashing lights. A few people came out of their houses to see what the commotion was about and whispered to one another, wondering what had happened. One of the police officers approached Ted, another instructed bystanders to stay back, and a third began placing a barricade tape across the bushes and around the area where Owen lay on the grass. The ambulance had arrived and was parked by the curb with flashing red lights.

An officer approached Ted. "I'm Officer Jefferson. I need to ask you a few questions, if you don't mind."

"Okay," Ted said.

"Your name, sir?"

"Ted Wyman." Ted had never had any interaction with the police.

"Your address, date of birth, and telephone number?" Jefferson wrote on a notepad as Ted spoke.

Ted didn't know why this was necessary but didn't want to argue.

"Are you the owner of this dog?"

"Yes, sir."

"And you were the one who called nine one one?"

When Ted answered in the affirmative, Jefferson asked

him to tell him what he saw.

"Well, I was walking my dog as I do every day." Ted spoke slowly, as if he was trying to recollect the scene. "Owen had waved at me from over there." Ted pointed in the direction. "I didn't realize when Dusti, my dog, slipped away from me. I had just received a phone call. I watched Owen run after him. Then a car whizzed past, and I saw Owen jump. The car sped away. By the time I reached Owen, he was lying here."

"Did you notice anything about the car or the driver? Can you give us any details?" Officer Jefferson continued.

"It looked like a late model, gray American sedan. I only saw the license plate briefly as I was crossing the street. I don't remember the complete sequence. There was a T and S and, I believe, two 7s at the end. It might have been a New York license plate, but I'm not sure. It seemed like the driver had a dark complexion and was wearing a black jacket. It happened so fast, I can't remember everything."

Jefferson thanked Ted and said he would get back to him later for more information, if needed. He then joined the other officers who were talking to the people gathered.

The paramedics were examining Owen when Agnes reached the scene.

"Oh my God. What happened?" She ran past the officers, but Jefferson restrained her.

"Let me see him. I'm his wife," she cried, trying to get

away.

"You will, you will. Just a few minutes, ma'am."

Noticing Ted she asked, "Ted, what happened?"

Ted repeated what he had told Jefferson. Agnes stood close to him, pressing the palm of her left hand and staring in the direction of Owen.

When the paramedics placed Owen on a stretcher, they allowed her to come close. She held Owen's hand as she walked alongside the stretcher, tears rolling down her cheeks. The paramedics had put an oxygen mask over Owen's nose.

"Hang in there, honey. You'll be all right," Agnes said softly. As they were closing the door of the ambulance, Ted approached her and said he would join her at the hospital. She held Owen's hand as they drove to the Huntington Hospital.

Chapter 54

While the doctors examined Owen, Ted and Agnes waited anxiously in a waiting room situated in a corner down the hallway. The room had two tables with chairs around them and a small sofa toward the wall. A small kitchen counter had a coffee pot, sugar packets, and a jar of Coffee-Mate. There was a vending machine close by with snacks.

Ted asked Agnes if she wanted a cup of coffee. "I'm okay," she replied.

A middle-aged couple had occupied a table closer to the counter. The man had a cup of coffee in his hand. They were not talking, just sitting there. A nurse came and asked them to follow her.

A few visitors walked past the waiting-room door, but there was not much activity. Once in a while, Agnes could hear chatter from the nurses' station and a page for a doctor.

The silence aggravated Agnes. Occasionally she took a deep breath and sighed. Ted walked away for a while and returned few minutes later.

"Any news?" he asked.

"No," Agnes replied. "Maybe I should ask the nurse. Why is it taking so long?" She got up and started pacing the small room.

After almost two hours, the attending emergency-room physician, Dr. Epstein, came in. The look on his face told Agnes that it wasn't going to be good news.

"We did all we could. I'm sorry," Epstein said with a serious face as he approached Agnes. "Dr. Martin had severe internal bleeding caused by blunt force trauma. He probably hit the curb or was hit by the car. We'll know more after the autopsy."

Agnes looked down. Ted put his arm around her shoulder. Tears flowed down her cheeks.

Agnes wanted to see Owen. Dr. Epstein asked her to follow him. Ted stayed behind. When she returned he hugged her again and took her home.

The house had suddenly taken an eerie feeling for Agnes. Ted's wife, Sylvia, came over with some food. Ted called Owen's office, Sally, and Dana. Word had spread in the neighborhood, and neighbors started coming in to express their sympathy to Agnes. Agnes talked with each of them in a calm voice. She still couldn't believe what had happened.

Next morning a story ran on the second page of the *Long Island Newsday* about the accident:

Prominent Doctor Involved in Hit and Run

Dr. Owen Martin, a prominent local pediatrician, was

apparently hit by a car as he ran in the vicinity of his home. Dr. Martin, 61, of the Dix Hills, Huntington, neighborhood was on his daily route through the neighborhood. He was taken to the Huntington Hospital emergency room where he later died.

The driver left the scene of the accident, but a witness, Ted Wyman, had noted partial numbers from the license plate. Nassau County police have requested people in the neighborhood to call them if they had witnessed anything specific. No charges have been filed yet. The authorities are investigating all possible leads and motives. Survivors are his wife Agnes and daughter Sally.

The funeral was simple. Ted offered a moving eulogy saying how even in his death; Owen showed his compassion and helpfulness toward his friends and fellow human beings. Sally and Dana came and stayed with Agnes for a week.

Chapter 55

Interstate 495, called the Long Island Expressway or LIE by the local residents, stretches from the Queens-Midtown Tunnel in Manhattan to the eastern most town of Riverhead, a distance of seventy miles. It is the major artery that carries daily commuters from Long Island to Manhattan and other surrounding boroughs. Because it is perpetually clogged by heavy traffic both ways, it is also known as the longest parking lot in the nation.

Demond got up early, skipped breakfast, and headed off on his mission to deliver a package of cannabis to Owen in Huntington. Owen had called requesting additional supply.

"The pouch you gave me was of immense help," Owen had said. "My ache was alleviated. I feel much better."

Demond was not familiar with the Long Island suburbs. On top of that, he wasn't used to driving a car. Owen had told him that meeting at a designated place along his running route was the best bet to exchange the package.

Demond didn't own a car. He didn't need one. Everything was accessible via the subway in New York City. He rented a car from a Budget rent-a-car dealer in Brooklyn. He checked the traffic report on the radio and knew that he had no choice but to slog through the forty-mile distance to reach Huntington. He fidgeted with the knobs on the dashboard to get familiar with the features of the rental car. He took the Brooklyn Queens Expressway and then merged onto the LIE. He was uneasy driving in the bumper-to-bumper traffic. In spite of the GPS on his smartphone, it was not easy to follow the directions given by the GPS lady. He looked for the Huntington off-ramp—Exit 49, leading to Route 110, but ended up taking the one going south instead of north. He should have merged earlier into the right lane, but nobody would allow him to change lanes, and by the time he saw the exit it, was too late.

"Typical New Yorkers," he muttered.

"In five hundred feet, make a legal U-turn," instructed the lady on the GPS.

"What's wrong with me today?" murmured Demond. He was worried that he might miss Owen. When he entered Grossman Street in the upper-middle-class Dix Hills neighborhood, he slowed down and kept looking for anyone running and anyone resembling Owen. The streets were lined with two-story colonial homes with well-manicured lawns. *It's so much nicer here than Brooklyn*, Demond thought.

A block away he noticed Owen running toward him to his left. He picked up his speed a bit to wave and to let him know that he had arrived as promised. Before he could do that, Owen dashed across the street in front of him, chasing a dog. Demond tried to maneuver his car to avoid hitting him, but it was too late. Before his foot hit the brake, Demond heard a terrible thump. He didn't look back. He knew what that sound meant. He just took off straight ahead.

"Oh my God, oh my God!" Demond cried, gasping for air. "What have I done? Oh, please God, save him. I didn't mean to hit him."

Under normal circumstances he would have stopped his car and got out to help. But he couldn't take the chance of being caught carrying a banned substance. He had always been so careful—and lucky, one might say—during the times he'd smuggled cannabis from Africa.

As he was leaving the neighborhood, he saw, in his rearview mirror, a man running toward Owen. He started to sweat a bit. There was no sense driving around without knowing where he was. What if someone noticed him and notified the authorities? When he hit Owen, there had been no one on the street whom he could see, except the one man. But whoever he was, he'd seemed focused on the man who'd been struck down. Demond was sure there would be an investigation and, sooner or later, they would come after him. The police had their ways. He needed to act fast and get out of there.

Demond drove a couple of miles north and made a left turn on Jericho Turnpike. A police cruiser, its lights flashing, was following him. The officer was waving his hands, asking Demond to pull over to the side.

I'm dead, thought Demond. *I didn't think they would act*

so fast.

The officer approached him as he pulled over to the side of the road. The traffic was heavy on both sides.

"Anything the matter, Officer?" Demond pulled down the driver's side window and tried not to appear nervous.

To his surprise, the officer didn't ask him for his driver license and registration, as they normally did.

"Not really," said the officer. "I wanted to let you know that you are dragging a long tree branch. Looks like it's stuck to your muffler. It could be dangerous."

"Thanks. At least it's not a dead body." Demond tried to make a joke out of it but suddenly realized that it wasn't the right thing to say.

The officer smiled, said to take care, and left. "That was a close call," Demond muttered.

He got out and removed the branch. As he merged back into traffic, he saw a small strip mall ahead. He was hungry since he had missed his breakfast. The mall had a Home Depot, a twenty-four-seven diner, a barbershop, and a UPS store. There was a space right in front of the diner, where he parked his car. A police patrol car came around and parked next to him. Demond looked at the officer and smiled. The officer nodded in return. It was the same officer that had stopped him. *Is he following me?* Demond wondered.

Demond went inside. He was greeted by a smiling young waitress, a brunette wearing a beige uniform and a white apron. She appeared to be in her late twenties or early thirties. The tag on her dress said, "Lydia."

"Good morning. How's your day going so far? Table for one?"

"Yes, please," Demond said softly, looking away from her without saying anything about how his day was going.

She took him to a booth and handed him a four-page menu that had items for breakfast, lunch, and dinner. The officer, probably on his break, sat at a counter across from Demond's booth.

Demond faced a long counter with revolving stools in front of the cooking station. He could see the police officer. A painter with white overalls was sitting in one corner, sipping coffee, and chatting with another waitress—a woman who looked older than Lydia.

"These kids think they are grown up and know everything," the waitress was telling the painter.

From what he'd overheard, Demond surmised that her daughter, a senior in high school, wanted to move out and live with her boyfriend. The painter was nodding in agreement.

Demond heard the sizzle from the grill as the short-order cook sprayed water and scraped the grill.

"Take your time," Lydia said when she came to take his order. Demond kept turning the pages from the menu, not sure what he wanted to order. After another moment, she walked away but soon returned.

"I just want a glazed doughnut and coffee, please. Sugar but no milk," he finally said. He gave the menu back to her.

"Will do."

Lydia took the menu and walked away. An old couple occupied another booth across from Demond. They were eating their breakfast slowly without talking. The man's hand shook whenever he lifted the fork to his lips. His companion just kept looking at him as she sipped coffee from a white mug.

As he waited for his coffee and doughnut, Demond thought of calling his wife, Gina. He had met Gina on a flight from Africa to the United States. She was volunteering as a nurse in Zambia. Their friendship grew, and they were married two years after their first meeting. They did not have any children.

Demond tapped Gina's number as he glanced at the officer, who nodded at him, and Owen nodded back. *Was it a friendly gesture from the officer or an attempt at keeping tabs on him?*

"Hi, babe, how's it going?" Demond said in a hushed voice when she answered. She had reported for work at the hospital. It was just after nine in the morning.

"Demond, why are you calling? You are all right?" Gina asked.

"Yes...I mean...uh, oh yes. I'm fine. Just thought of talking with you and hearing your voice."

"You had your meeting with whomever?"

"Yes...I mean...no. It was at ten. I was on my way," Demond stuttered. "But he canceled...yes, canceled...at the last minute."

"Demond, you don't sound right. What's going on?"

"I'm fine. I'm fine. I'll come home early, and maybe we can go out to eat somewhere."

"That'll be super."

"Love you," he said as he hung up.

"Love you too."

Chapter 56

Demond wished he had talked longer with Gina, but he didn't know what to talk about. He didn't want to tell her what had happened that morning. He just needed to make a contact with someone and hear someone's voice. But she had work to do, and he knew he shouldn't keep her on the phone.

The coffee and doughnut were waiting for him. The police officer had left. Demond felt queasy in his stomach. The coffee had already gotten cold. The old couple stood up and left.

Demond spent an hour in the coffee shop, hoping the traffic on the expressway would lighten up. He asked for refills twice. After leaving the diner, he drove straight back toward Brooklyn. He turned the radio to WINS, the CBS news station for all the news all the time, to see if there was an update on his accident. The noise of the commercial trucks drowned the voice from the radio. Some crazy drivers were weaving in and out of the lanes. He shook his head, turned off the radio, and slapped the passenger seat in frustration. He was exhausted by the time he reached Brooklyn. His head ached. He returned the rental car and walked back to his apartment.

Two days after his trip to Huntington, the *New York Daily News* had a report about the suspicious death of a well-known pediatrician on Long Island. The story on the fourth page said:

Dr. Owen Martin, a noted pediatrician, was hit by a car as he ran in the Dix Hills neighborhood in Huntington, Long Island, where he lived. The driver left the scene of the accident. Dr. Martin's neighbor, who was walking his dog, noted partial numbers from the license plate of the car. Dr. Martin was taken to the Huntington Hospital emergency room where he died a while later. The Nassau County police have no details about the driver of the car, other than the fact that it was a dark-complected man who is alleged to have killed Dr. Martin.

Dr. Martin had gained reputation when he was listed as one of the top fifty physicians on Long Island. He is survived by his wife, Agnes, and daughter, Sylvia.

The investigation continues.

His eyes swelled with tears as he read the report. He didn't want Gina to notice him crying, and he also didn't want her to read the news. He tore the page, got up, and threw it in the garbage. He went upstairs to the bathroom and splashed cold water on his face. He was sure that sooner or later the authorities would track him down.

That afternoon Demond collected the supply of cannabis from his home and, without Gina's knowledge, took it to the auto dealership to hide it in a far corner in the parts department. Demond was working as a salesman at a Ford dealership to supplement his work at Spice of Life. It was not the best place to hide, but it was safer than his house, in case he got raided by the police.

Ever since his return from Long Island, Demond had been lost in his thoughts. He feared that Gina might have noticed his unusual lack of bubbly demeanor. During dinner he didn't tell her about his day at the dealership, nor did he ask her how her day was at the hospital.

He complained about heartburn quite often, which Gina said worried her. But Demond ignored her pleas to see a doctor. She finally gave up, saying she hoped it was something that would go away over time.

"Should we go to a movie this weekend?" Gina asked one day.

Demond suggested that they just stay home.

Once in a while, he would get up, walk over to the window facing the street, and look outside.

"You are expecting someone?" she would ask.

"No, no. Just watching people walk around. I wonder what they are up to. Are they all going shopping perhaps or walking to the subway to go to Manhattan?"

Gina didn't seem convinced. She thought perhaps he was being unduly pressured by his boss to increase sales. Thankfully, she didn't press him for an explanation and went about doing chores in the house or planning an event in her church. But she could tell he wasn't a happy camper.

Chapter 57

Officer Martingale of the Nassau County Police
Department (NCPD) didn't have much to go on in investigating
the hit-and-run accident that killed Dr. Owen Martin. Information
provided by the neighbor wasn't enough to track down the car
involved. It could have been driven by anyone—someone living in
the neighborhood rushing to go to work, a visitor from out of state,
or a landscaper. There were no clues except for the partial plate
numbers. The Department of Motor Vehicles had a backlog and
was going to take a few days to check those.

Martingale assigned officers to interview the residents of
the Dix Hills in the immediate neighborhood of Owen's residence.
The preliminary autopsy had reported finding traces of marijuana
in Owen's blood. Was Owen going to rendezvous with a dealer?
What and how much did Agnes know? It was a standard police
legwork.

A week had passed before Martingale got a call from the
New York Police Department (NYPD). The Brooklyn Budget rent-
a-car office had informed the NYPD that they had discovered a
package of marijuana in one of the cars they had rented to a
Demond Ibori. The numbers on the rental car plate were similar to
some of the numbers reported in published reports. Officer

Martingale called the car-rental office.

"Yes," said the agent when Martingale reached him. "A bag of cannabis was found in a car we had rented out."

"Really? When was the car rented?" he asked.

The date provided by the agent matched the date of the hit-and-run accident.

"Got any more details?" Martingale continued.

"The car was rented to another person the same day, and he drove it across the country. We didn't check the car thoroughly to see if anything was left back; we should have. The person who returned the car today told us."

"Can you tell us about the car and the license plate?"

"Gray Ford Escort with license plate number TS9577."

"Who rented the car the first time?"

"A Mr. Demond Ibori. He listed his address in Brooklyn, New York."

"Go on, please."

"I read the story about the doctor's death in a hit-and-run case. The car was rented on the night prior to the date of the accident and was returned sooner than the estimated time. And now, the discovery of the drugs! We have no way of knowing where the car was driven. I wonder if the doctor was involved with some shady characters."

"Possible. But it's a long shot," Martingale said. He didn't want to tell the agent about the forensic report.

"By the way," he continued. "Did Mr. Ibori rent a GPS from you guys?"

"No, he didn't."

Martingale thanked him. He had a new lead. If Demond had rented a GPS from Budget, it would have provided information on the routes he had taken. Perhaps he used the map function from his own smartphone, but there was no way of knowing.

Martingale poured himself a cup of coffee, walked back to his desk, and retrieved the file with the neighbor's interview. The man had mentioned the car was a gray late-model American car with the license plate that had letters T and S and two 7s at the end. He wondered if Owen might be involved in drug trafficking. He had to talk to Agnes.

Chapter 58

Agnes received a call from the police asking for an appointment. The officer apologized for the inconvenience during her period of mourning but said new information received from the NYPD needed confirmation.

Officer Martingale and his assistant arrived two days later. Agnes verified their identity and escorted them in. She pointed to a sofa facing the bay window in the small living room. Martingale looked to be in his late fifties, probably a veteran of the police force, Agnes thought. He introduced his companion to Agnes, but she soon forgot the name. Martingale and his companion walked past a hallway decorated with family pictures and sat on the sofa. Agnes sat across from them in a large chair and clasped her hands together. She was calm as she braced herself for a barrage of questions.

Martingale cleared his throat. "We apologize for the inconvenience, Mrs. Martin. I'll try to be brief."

"Thank you," Agnes said, almost in a whisper.

"Let's start with Dr. Martin. What kind of practice did he have?"

"Pediatric."

"And was his practice limited to Huntington?"

"Strictly Huntington."

"Did anyone from out of state visit him recently?"

"Not that I know of."

"Where has Dr. Martin been lately, other than on local travels?" Martingale's tone was matter of fact. His assistant was taking notes.

"Nowhere really," Agnes replied. She glanced out the bay window as if to recollect something, and then said, "Oh, I just remembered we visited Montego Bay, Jamaica, earlier this year."

"Vacation or business?"

"Well, both, really. Owen participated in a panel discussion at the All American Pediatric Association convention."

"Did either of you meet anyone suspicious there?"

"Well, I don't think so. He was busy with the convention during the day, but at night we were always together."

"And you didn't meet anyone else, and no one else tried to contact Dr. Martin?"

"We did meet a Professor Ashley and his wife when we were waiting for our flight back."

"Professor Ashley?"

"Yes. He and Owen had attended University of Oklahoma

together. Dr. Ashley is a professor at University of Michigan."

"Thank you." Martingale's assistant wrote something in his notebook. Martingale continued his questioning, further probing Owen's connection to out-of-town people.

"Did you notice any change in Dr. Martin's behavior in the last few weeks?"

"No, he was busy with his practice and came home after his work. He was disciplined and followed his daily routine. He was a Vietnam War veteran," Agnes replied, with pride in her voice.

Owen had maintained, she told him, his normal habit of running every morning. He had been a good husband and a devoted father.

"Do you have any children, Mrs. Martin?"

"Our daughter, Sally, lives in Commack. She is married."

"Anyone else?"

"His sister, Dana, lives in Manhasset with her husband, Roger."

"I see. Do you know of any people Dr. Martin knew in New York City?"

"No."

"Anyone besides close family? Friends or people he might have come across in his business or otherwise?"

"Let me see," Agnes responded reflectively. "He and Roger visited a bar in Lower Manhattan few months ago. But that was not to visit any friend."

"What was it for? Just two grown men hanging out in the Big Apple?"

"No. I want to be truthful, Officer. Owen suffered from a debilitating condition. A chiropractor had recommended he try taking marijuana to see if it might relieve the pain."

"Thank you for volunteering the information, Mrs. Martin. We are trying to figure out if Dr. Martin had any dealings with suspicious characters, for instance."

"I can assure you my husband was not associated with a drug ring. He was a good Christian. We went to church every Sunday. He led an honest and clean life." Agnes tried to speak as calmly as she could.

"We don't doubt that, Mrs. Martin. We just have to be sure. We have come to know that the person who hit your husband was carrying a package of marijuana in his car, and he had listed his address in New York. Preliminary autopsy showed traces of marijuana in Dr. Martin's blood."

Agnes just stared at him. She knew of Owen's visit to the hookah bar in New York City.

"Yes. That's possible. He had bought a small quantity at a bar during his visit to New York City," she said after a pause.

"But it is an illegal substance, Mrs. Martin."

"It may be. He was only using it for medical purposes. He was not a drug addict."

"Thank you, Mrs. Martin. If you remember anything, please call. Here's my card, just in case." Martingale and his assistant got up to leave. She had admitted Owen's possession of an illegal substance, which could be a crime. Was there a chance she could be incriminated as an accomplice? She didn't care. The use of marijuana had helped Owen, and she was prepared to defend it to whoever wanted to listen.

Chapter 59

Agnes sat in her chair for a while, staring out the window. She knew Martingale was not through with the investigation. He would return, possibly with a search warrant. She decided to look into Owen's computer to see if she could find anything about Owen's connections she was unaware of. She had her own laptop, which she used for e-mail and shopping, but had never thought of snooping into Owen's computer.

She went into the study and closed the door to avoid being disturbed by the phone ringing in the kitchen. With no idea what she was looking for, she felt awkward and uncomfortable digging into her husband's private life.

The computer was password protected. She tried several combinations—their names, birthdates, numbers from their home address, contraction of his business name, and so on. Nothing worked. To ward off the frustration, she walked over to the kitchen and poured a glass of cold water from the refrigerator water dispenser. She stared out of the kitchen window for a long time. Finally, as she walked back to the study, she remembered Owen was from Pauls Valley, Oklahoma. *It's worth a try*, she thought. The acronym Pvok, Pauls Valley, Oklahoma, was close enough. Agnes added Owen's birth year at the end, separated by an ampersand. Lo and behold, she got lucky.

The computer had the usual folders—pictures, videos, music, and documents. Under documents were several draft letters, notes for the conference, and Turbo Tax files. Then under a folder called *My Diary,* subfolders with dates in their names went back to her days in Malawi. *That's interesting,* Agnes thought. Owen had always been open with her. What could be in these files? And why had he kept them secret from her?

The folders were a kind of journal that Owen had written over the years, arranged in chronological order, starting with his years in Malawi as a Peace Corps volunteer until two days before his death. Agnes started reading from the beginning.

I am so excited to start my assignment as a PCV. There are numerous challenges in the work I have been assigned.

A little later he mentioned meeting Rachel, a fellow volunteer, and expressed concern about her health.

I really like being with Rachel. I hope she gets used to the food here and stops being sick all the time.

The memories of her volunteer days in Malawi filled Agnes with sadness. She had lived with Rachel and enjoyed her friendship, but when Rachel left because of bad health and trauma from the hoodlums' attack, she had felt bad. They stayed in contact for a few years until Rachel stopped responding and Agnes gave up. When in Malawi, Agnes never dreamt that she would marry Owen. He was friends with Rachel, and she had left it at that.

It's sad that Demond stole the mosquito nets. I blame the company he keeps. He is a nice young boy, and I should help him.

Agnes hadn't been aware that Owen had met Demond in Malawi.

By noon Agnes was hungry but didn't feel like making a sandwich. She ate a banana and drank orange juice. She went back to read more of Owen's diary. After a while she started skipping the earlier entries and went straight to the current files.

The diary had entries about Owen's struggle with chronic back pain.

I have seen all the experts about my back pain. No one seems to know what's going on. I am going to take the advice of Rodriguez, the chiropractor.

He wrote how glad he was that he got reacquainted with Demond at the hookah bar in Manhattan. He couldn't restrain his joy at meeting an old acquaintance from Malawi.

It was a blessing that I ran into Demond, of all the people, in Spice of Life. I am glad he was able to get out of his miserable life in Malawi and make something for himself. Although I don't approve of the profession he has chosen.

Owen had made arrangements with Demond to receive packets of the cannabis. She found nothing to connect Demond to a drug ring.

The mail usually arrived at two o'clock. At half past two,

Agnes took a break and walked over to the mailbox at the end of her long driveway. As usual the mail was mostly junk—brochures from cruise lines, an invitation for magazine subscriptions, and coupons for handyman and window-washing services. There were a couple of bills, which she kept in the study after putting the due date on the envelope.

It was way past six o'clock in the evening when Agnes closed the computer with a long sigh. It was October. The days were getting shorter, and it was getting dark earlier. She came out of the study and walked to the kitchen. The red light on the telephone base pad was blinking. She listened to a message from Sally, followed by two robo calls from telemarketers. She deleted them.

She called Sally and told her that she had dozed off and didn't hear the phone ringing. Sally was worried about her mom and wanted Agnes to move in to stay with her.

"You can have all the privacy you want. You can have your own room. You can cook if you want. Do whatever. The local library has a book club, where you could meet new people."

"I am fine here, Sally," Agnes replied calmly. "For now, at least. Besides I have to take care of your father's papers and stuff—close all the accounts, hand over the practice to a new buyer, if there is going to be one."

"But you are all by yourself."

"I'm not that far from you, Sally. Commack is less than

half-hour drive."

Sally didn't push any further.

That evening Agnes didn't feel like doing anything. She didn't want to cook. Ordering takeout from the local China Garden was an easier choice. She liked hot-and-sour soup, Hunan style chicken, and shrimp Lo Mein with extra hot sauce on the side. Somehow she had a sudden craving for hot and spicy food. She had a bottle of Chianti, already open.

She poured some wine in a glass and picked a piece of chicken with a fork right out of the carton. A few minutes later, she walked to the study. Owen's picture, taken when he was recognized as one of Long Island's fifty best physicians, was on the bookcase. Agnes picked it up and brought it to the kitchen. Her eyes became moist as she kept staring at the picture, and hiccupped. A tear dropped on the glass. She wiped it away with her hand.

Half the Chinese food was left on the table. She had no appetite. There was nothing on TV. After Owen's death she only watched the news and occasionally Larry King. She was trying to get used to living by herself. It was hard. The big house was empty. She missed him.

Agnes sipped the wine. There were two fortune cookies next to the Lo Mein. She opened one of them.

The greatest risk is not taking one.

She tore it to pieces and tossed it on the table next to the food. When she lifted the bottle by its neck and looked at the bottom, it was empty.

"I guess that's enough for today," she muttered. "What I need is a warm bath." She ran the Jacuzzi and soaked herself in hot water. The vapors from the water soothed her. She slept within a few minutes of retiring to her bed.

The next day at breakfast, Agnes scanned the *Newsday*. There were no updates to Owen's story. *How soon the world forgets*, she thought. Agnes sensed that this was a lull before the storm.

She didn't know why, but she thought of Ashley and his wife, Samantha, whom she had met at the Montego Bay airport and their invitation to visit them at Thanksgiving. Agnes remembered Ashley had mentioned that he had noticed Owen because of the *OU* baseball cap Owen always wore.

"Ashley must be expecting us for Thanksgiving," she said to herself. "I must inform him about Owen's sudden death." She mailed the cap to Ashley with a short note informing him about Owen's accidental death and the reason for sending the cap—*It was because of the cap that the two of you recognized each other at the Montego Bay Airport,* she wrote.

Chapter 60

Samantha was in her kitchen, savoring her second cup of coffee while reading the morning paper. It was that moment of quiet that she treasured most. Ashley had left for the university. He taught a nine o'clock class. Those were the few hours she used to organize and plan the rest of the day. She sometimes ran errands, did the laundry, or called her friend Courtney to chat. The day was hers till three o'clock, when Ashley usually dropped by for an hour or so before returning for his graduate seminar or to supervise the students working under him for their doctorates.

There was a knock on the front door. Samantha ignored it, thinking it to be a door-to-door salesman or someone looking for donations to a charity. But why would they come so early in the morning? Ashley and Samantha owned a charming, medium-sized, colonial house just outside the Ann Arbor campus. The closest neighbors were about twenty feet away. There had been no reported robberies or vandalism in the vicinity. *Still, it's better to be careful*, she thought. It was broad daylight, and she knew Courtney would be at home. In case she shouted she would be within hearing range. Still, her mind was occupied by thoughts that strange things could occur in unsuspected places.

When the knocking persisted, she walked to the door and

peered through the keyhole. A man dressed in casual business attire was standing on the stoop with his back to the door. He was looking away at the house across the street. She opened the door with a bit of trepidation.

"May I help you?" she asked.

He turned and smiled as he handed her his business card and said, "Connor. Connor Flaherty, from the FBI. You have a couple of minutes?"

Samantha hesitated as she took his card. What could this be? Was Ashley in trouble for something he did at the university? He always confided in her and told her everything about his work. Perhaps one of his students was in trouble with the law. She was not aware of any of her neighbors involved in illegal activities, in case they were under investigation. Or maybe there was a robbery in the neighborhood.

"Do you have any identification?" she asked. She wanted something more official than his business card.

"Yes, of course."

He reached for his wallet and pulled out a credit card-like badge.

She was not sure if she should invite the man inside. He saved her by clarifying. "I am really looking for Dr. Wilkins. Is he home, or should I come some other time?"

"Most mornings, he is at the university. Would you like to

visit him there?"

"Well, I tell you what. You can have him call me at his convenience. My number is listed on my card."

"What's this about?" Samantha asked, showing concern.

"I would really like to talk to him personally," the FBI agent said calmly, without displaying any emotion.

"Okay."

After he'd left, Samantha had a feeling that it was something illegal and hoped Ashley was not in any trouble with the law. First she thought she could wait until he made his afternoon visit to tell him about the FBI showing up at their house. But curiosity took over. She called Ashley at his office but only got his answering machine. She left a message that he should call her immediately on an important matter. An hour went by but there was no call.

Probably still in his class, she thought. *Should I just drive over and tell him in person? Be patient, Samantha. It's not the end of the world.* She thought of calling Courtney, but it wasn't something she wanted to talk with her about.

"What's wrong, Samantha? You never call me at my office," Ashley said when he finally called at eleven thirty. "What's so important?"

Samantha told him about the FBI agent's visit and asked if he was in any kind of trouble.

"I'll be damned if I know what they want," he said, sounding a bit agitated. "Did he leave his number?"

"Yes. He gave me his card. Do you want it now?"

"No. It can wait. I'll take a look when I stop by this afternoon."

When he came home that afternoon, Samantha handed him the card. Ashley looked at it carefully. He turned it back and forth as if there might be more information on the other side. He put it in the front pocket of his shirt.

"Don't lose it," Samantha warned. She was aware that lately Ashley was losing track of where he has kept things. "It's not Alzheimer's," he'd said many times, in jest.

"I'll be careful."

Ashley was curious too. He called the number on the card immediately. A voice mail instructed him to leave a message. Ashley left word that he would call the next day, and he specified a time after his morning classes.

Chapter 61

During his class the next morning, Ashley's mind was on Connor's visit. He ignored students with raised hands wanting to ask him questions, continuing with his lecture instead. After class, a student wanted to discuss something, but Ashley asked him to come back later. Once in his office, he closed the door. He didn't want any interruptions when he was talking with Connor. His office was small with a desk facing the window and a bookcase toward the wall. Stacks of papers were piled up on the table. He could see students walking outside. Ashley settled into his chair, put his feet on the table, and called Flaherty. A receptionist answered and transferred the call.

"I know you are a busy man, Dr. Wilkins. I won't take much of your time. I just have a few questions for you," the agent said.

Ashley was expecting the typical bureaucrat—arrogant, condescending. Instead, the agent was polite.

"Shoot."

"We are contacting you with regard to an ongoing investigation about a hit-and-run accident on Long Island, New York. This is at the request of the Nassau County, LI police department."

"Okay."

"Did you know a Dr. Owen Martin?"

"Yes. I know a Dr. Owen Martin from Huntington. Yes."

"Precisely, what was the nature of your acquaintance?"

"I've known Owen since we were both students at the University of Oklahoma."

"Did you continue to be in touch with him after you both graduated from the university?"

Ashley didn't understand why the officer was asking about his deceased friend.

"Not really. Owen, uh...Dr. Martin...left to join the military. Then he did a stint as a Peace Corps Volunteer in Malawi, Africa."

"Were you in touch with him during his tour of duty at the Peace Corps?"

"Not all the time."

Ashley said the only letter he had received from Owen from Malawi included a photo of him with a young lady, whose name he didn't remember.

"What else do you know about Dr. Martin as a Peace Corps volunteer?"

"Not much. Not much at all. Is he in some kind of trouble?"

The agent didn't answer the question. "Did Dr. Martin tell you about a Demond Ibori?"

"Demond Ibori? No, I've no idea who he is or what he has to do with Owen." Ashley answered, pausing between each sentence as if to think it over.

"You know about Dr. Martin's death?"

"Yes."

"How did you hear about Dr. Martin's death?"

"I'd invited him and his wife Agnes to visit us for Thanksgiving. That never happened. According to Agnes's note, he died as a result of a freak accident when he was running near his home."

"That's right. Did Mrs. Martin say anything more?"

"No. She sent me the baseball cap that Owen always wore."

"Thank you, Dr. Wilkins. Are you still in possession of the cap?"

"Of course! That was Owen's trademark. I have kept it in a prominent place in my study."

"Thank you, again. You have been really helpful. I'll be in touch if I need more information. Have a nice remainder of the day."

With that the agent hung up the phone. Ashley didn't have a chance to reciprocate, not that he really had anything to add.

Ashley put his legs down and straightened himself in his chair. He looked out the window and wondered why his caller had thanked him. Was it just to be polite? He really didn't give the man any worthwhile information, at least, not that it appeared to him. Their conversation went smoother than he'd expected, but as he thought more about it, it became obvious that there was something behind all those questions about Owen. *Demond Ibori? What was between him and Owen?*

That afternoon, Ashley related the phone conversation to Samantha. She was as perplexed as he. The only thing they could do was to wait and see if they would hear from the FBI again.

Ashley peeked inside his study. The baseball cap with the *OU* logo and the name *Owen* under it was still there. Ashley suspected that it had some significance in Owen's life, more than he ever knew or imagined. Otherwise why would anyone be interested to know if he still had the cap?

Chapter 62

It had been a month since Owen's death, and no one had contacted Demond. He and his wife, Gina, went about their daily routine—he at the car dealership and she at the hospital. The topic of his visit to Long Island rarely came up in their conversation. There was no reason for it. Gina took Demond at his word that his meeting never took place and he had to return home early.

Then one Saturday, when they had finished their breakfast and retreated to the living room, Gina saw a Chevrolet Impala pull into their driveway. They rarely got visitors this early in the morning on weekends. She knew the cars their friends drove. This was not one of them. She asked Demond if he was expecting someone. He said no. But he had a suspicion that the time had come.

When the doorbell rang, Gina looked through the peephole. Two men stood on the stoop—one standing nearly six feet tall and the other, a shorter man. Both wore police uniforms. She hesitated to open the door to these law enforcement officers but felt secure since Demond was home. Opening the front door just so the security chain was engaged, she addressed the men waiting outside.

"How may I help you?" she asked.

"Yes, ma'am. Is this the residence of Mr. Demond Ibori?"

"Yes, it is. Is anything the matter? I'm his wife."

"NYPD. We would like to ask Mr. Ibori some questions." She had no idea what this was about. The taller one introduced himself as John and pointed to the shorter one, who he said was Mike.

Gina didn't know what to do. She had never faced a situation like this. Should she let them in? She wished Demond was with her.

The officers noticed her hesitation. They pulled out their identification badges and showed them to Gina. She showed them inside and pointed to a sofa for them to take a seat.

"Demond, Demond. There's someone to see you."

She went back to the kitchen and peeked in other rooms, but there was no sign of Demond. She guessed he'd gone upstairs to use the bathroom. Her hands shook as she returned to the living room. Officers John and Mike were looking around the room as if they might discover a hidden artifact.

"He'll be here in a minute," she said, though she didn't know how long Demond would take.

Gina sat facing them, her eyes darting around the room. What should she say to fill the time? She adjusted the magazines on the table, neatly stacking them. A few awkward moments passed without anyone saying anything.

"We heard Mr. Ibori was visiting Long Island a short while ago," Officer Mike said, breaking the silence.

"Yes."

"How long was he there?"

So, this is about Demond's trip to Long Island, thought Gina. "It was a one-day business trip. He came home early because the other person canceled on him."

Something in the officers' expressions told Gina that she'd just given them information they'd come for. Now, she felt even more uncomfortable. If they asked her more questions, could she just refuse to answer?

"Do you have any idea what his trip was for?" Officer Mike asked.

"He's a car salesman. His boss sent him to meet a dealer."

Gina just made up an answer. Again, she thought Demond should have been there to answer the questions. Was he involved in buying or offloading cars illegally? She couldn't think of a sound reason. She wished he'd told her about it in more detail. *Where is Demond? Why isn't he here answering all these questions?*

A moment later she said, "He will be a better person to answer that. He'll be here in a minute, I'm sure."

When a few more minutes had passed, and there was no sign of her husband, she got worried.

"Pardon me a moment," she said as she got up. "I'll go see what's keeping him."

Gina went upstairs. He was not in their bedroom. Their bed was not made up yet. The bathroom door, just off their bedroom, was closed but not locked. Gina knocked on the door and called for Demond.

"Demond, are you in there? What's taking so long? The officers are waiting for you."

There was no answer. It wasn't like Demond. She opened the door a bit and peeked inside. She could see Demond's feet. She opened the door wider.

The officers downstairs heard a shriek that could be heard for a block. Officer John rushed upstairs. Gina knelt over Demond's body, sprawled on the bathroom rug, arms by his side, and eyes closed as if in deep sleep. He wasn't moving. The faucet from the sink dripped slowly. Gina cried loudly and uncontrollably.

Officer John was on his cell phone calling for an ambulance. He and Officer Mike took Demond to the Methodist Hospital, where Gina worked. Demond was taken to the emergency room. Gina and the officers waited in the lobby as doctors tried to revive him. John tried to console her. Tears trickled down her face as she tried to compose herself. She looked up as a young doctor in green scrubs walked up to her.

"Are you related to the patient?"

"Yes. I'm his wife," Gina said as he wiped her eyes. Although she worked at the hospital, not all the doctors knew her.

"We are sorry; we did all we could."

Gina remained quiet. The officers stayed in the background not wishing to interfere.

"Was he in pain? Did he suffer?" she asked.

"We think he suffered a cardiac arrest. Did he have a history of heart problems?"

Gina remembered Demond talking of heartburn and his frequently waking up at night. He had dismissed it, thinking the symptoms would vanish over time. She blamed herself for not insisting that he see a doctor.

The officers stayed with Gina at the hospital until she called her parents and friends. They left after telling her to call them if she needed any help. That was the least they could do. Now that Demond was dead, there was no way to interrogate him or charge him with a crime. It was not yet proven that he had hit Owen and left the scene.

Chapter 63

Agnes had never heard of an organization with the unusual name like NORML. She wanted to find out more. The article explained that the National Organization for the Reform of Marijuana Laws was committed to educate the communities in the benefits of the use of marijuana to help people suffering from debilitating health conditions. Their aim was not to encourage drug dealers but to help those in need. The article further stated:

We need volunteers to spread the word in your communities. Contact your representatives to enact laws, at least at the state level, to legalize controlled use of marijuana. Come help us. Call the number, and you will be glad you did.

Agnes closed her eyes when she finished reading. She folded the paper, went to the study, and lifted Owen's photo from the desk.

Tell me, Owen. What shall I do? I have never spoken in public or lobbied. It has been a long time since my work in Africa.

After a moment, this seemed like something he would want her to do.

Upon returning to the breakfast table, she took a deep breath. She looked at the clock. It was just past nine. Too early to call the NORML chapter. She didn't feel like reading the rest of the paper. She ate a slice of whole-wheat toast with peanut butter and finished her coffee.

While taking a shower, Agnes thought about the article she had read. She liked the idea of working to repeal the prohibition on the use of marijuana for medical purposes. If marijuana was legal and available in local drug stores, Owen wouldn't have had to go through back channels. Owen had been running the same route daily, and nothing had happened in all these years. It was because of the nonavailability of cannabis through legal channels that Owen had to have the man from the hookah bar come all the way to Long Island that resulted in his death.

I must do something, she said to herself. *I can speak from personal experience. It will certainly resonate with the people.*

That afternoon she called the number and registered her name to attend the next meeting.

Chapter 64

Officer Martingale was late coming to work. The traffic on the LIE had been bad, and some crazy person tried to cut in front of him, narrowly missing his front bumper. He had kept his cool. He needed a hot cup of coffee.

Samara, his secretary, was talking to someone on the phone. He wanted to ask her if the final autopsy report for the hit-and-run case involving Dr. Owen Martin had come from the Nassau County medical examiner. The preliminary hospital autopsy showed traces of marijuana in Owen's blood. But he was told the detailed official report would not be available until all the laboratory testing was complete. This could take several weeks. Preliminary background check on Demond indicated his birthplace as Malawi, Africa. Martingale had requested the FBI to get involved to see if international drug trafficking was involved.

He walked past her to the small kitchen, lifted a Styrofoam cup from the stack, and poured himself black coffee. He preferred it without the cream and sugar, especially today.

As he walked towards Samara she raised her right arm, continuing to talk on the phone. *Why do these ladies have to talk so early in the morning?* Martingale said to himself. He was not in a mood for small talk. When he approached her desk, she stopped talking, placed the phone on the base pad, and looked up at him.

"Anything important in the mail?" he asked.

"You mean the autopsy report for the Martin/Ibori case?"

"Uh. Huh."

"Sorry, nothing."

"Okay. Let me know when it comes in"

"Sure, will do."

Martingale walked to his desk and turned on his computer. He cursed the police department and wondered why they were so far behind in getting new, faster equipment. When it finally did come up, he clicked on the e-mail. There were a few inquiries on some past cases he had worked on. A message from the District Attorney inquiring about the Martin/Ibori case said:

A respected doctor from our community dies in a hit-and-run accident. No motive is evident except the discovery of marijuana in the car rented by the driver. Do we have proof that the doctor was a customer of Mr. Ibori? What is the latest on this? We need to answer this to the public as soon as we can.

Martingale was aware of the importance and urgency of closing the case as soon as possible. A lot depended on feedback from agents Connor Flaherty, Mike Garrison, and John Banks. Connor had interviewed Dr. Ashley Wilkins of the University of Michigan. Mike and John were in New York City talking with Ibori.

I like the challenge, Martingale said to himself. An e-mail from the medical examiner's office said, "We are aware of the urgency and are working as expeditiously as we can." It further said he can expect the autopsy report that afternoon. Martingale thought of calling Connor, Mike, and John but decided against it. He spent the rest of the morning reviewing Owen's file and his notes from the interview with Agnes. The local FBI agents had obtained a search warrant for Owen's computers.

The FBI forensic lab found a wealth of information on Owen's personal computer. The computer from his office had only patient information and data from his website.

Earlier entries in Owen's diary on his personal computer described his work as a Peace Corps Volunteer in Malawi:

I'm really enjoying my work at the Malawi clinic. Ms. Kasigo takes me with her to distribute the mosquito nets to the poor families. I think these families need more guidance on hygiene.

I'm really disappointed that Demond sold the nets given to his family. Apparently the money was more important to him than their health.

More recent entries showed issues with a chronic back pain and his attempt to alleviate the pain by using marijuana.

Such a big surprise to meet Demond at the hookah bar after all these years. It brought back memories of bygone days. The cannabis has definitely helped me. Demond has promised to supply the substance, in person if I so desire. I have to be discreet though.

"The good doctor was indeed a customer of Demond Ibori for the supply of cannabis, albeit for health reasons." Martingale murmured. "It is so unfortunate. The drug seems to have helped him, but it is still legally forbidden."

He read the report about the physical examination of the car that Demond had rented. It stated that the underside of the right bumper had grass clippings and shreds of plastic. Demond had hit something. The Nassau County police concluded that he must have hit a bag full of grass clippings. It was too late to examine the bags because they had been picked up by the trash collectors. The bumper had no trace of blood. The car was also rented to another person before it was inspected and could have picked up the debris from that trip.

Martingale closed the file at noon and walked over to the Burger King in the strip mall across the street. He wanted a quick lunch. Not that he had to make up for coming late that morning, but he had so much on his plate.

When he returned to his office, Samara was still out. He checked his e-mails again to see if there was anything new. He quickly glanced over the list of mail. There was nothing significant. As he closed the e-mail, an alert popped up on his screen. There was a new message from Connor Flaherty. Martingale clicked it open.

I had a nice talk with Professor Wilkins. In my opinion

Prof. Wilkins was not aware of the latest happenings in Dr. Martin's life. He had known Dr. Martin during his college days, but they were not in frequent touch with each other. They briefly met at the Montego Airport earlier this year, when Dr. Wilkins invited Dr. Martin to visit him for Thanksgiving. Dr. Wilkins was not aware of the circumstances of Dr. Martin's accident.

Someone tapped Martingale's shoulder. Samara had an envelope in her hand.

The autopsy report, six pages long, contained sections describing the many tests performed on the body and the conclusions—personal information of the deceased, external examination, pathological diagnoses, gross description, cause of death, summary, and manner of death.

Martingale flipped through the pages. The external examination noted scratches on the face, traces of blood, and a bump on the forehead. *He probably jumped to avoid the car coming at him and hit a tree stump or something,* thought Martingale.

The cause of death: blunt-force trauma. Manner of death: homicide.

A case was building up against Demond Ibori. Martingale still needed to hear from Mike and John from New York. He didn't want to call the DA's office before he had collected all the information.

At four thirty in the afternoon another message popped up

on his computer—an e-mail from John Banks. John described how their mission to talk with Demond turned futile due to his unexpected death. He said a detailed report would be prepared and that Martingale should expect it within a few days.

Martingale didn't know whether it was good news or bad news. There would be no trial since no one can be indicted.

Martingale yawned, got up from his chair, and stretched his arms behind his back.

"I'm tired," he said softly. "Tomorrow. Tomorrow I'll put everything together. I'll first call Agnes to inform her about the autopsy report, and then I'll call the DA."

He hoped tomorrow's commute wouldn't be as bad as today's.

Chapter 65

Martingale called Agnes as soon as he settled down in his office the next day. Her phone was busy. He didn't want to leave a message. *It's important I talk to her in person*, he thought, and decided to call her later.

Agnes had not talked with her daughter, Sally, for the past two weeks. She stopped eating her breakfast, put the newspaper aside, and called her.

"Mom, guess what?" Sally said excitedly before Agnes could say anything.

"*Don't* tell me," Agnes said.

"Yes. It's happening." Sally continued. "I had my appointment with Dr. Ngyun yesterday afternoon. She confirmed it. I'm going to be a mom, Mom. Isn't that great?"

"Congratulations. I'm really, really happy for you," Agnes said in a motherly tone. She wondered why Sally hadn't called her about the important event. "Now the fun starts. Oh, Sally. I remember when I was expecting with you. There is so much to plan and so much to do. I'm excited too."

"Mom, now you must move in with us. I'm really going to

need all the help I can get."

"You have a point. But there is something I haven't told you."

"What's that?"

"I've joined NORML as a volunteer."

"NORML?"

"Yes. It's an organization to lobby for the use of marijuana for medical purposes. If the drug was legalized, your dad wouldn't have had to go through the back channel to get it. Oh, Sally, I feel so strongly about this."

"You seem to be really committed."

"Yes. I think it's a way I can redeem your dad's death and hopefully help others in the future. He was in such a pain before he started using the drug. I think the government should take notice of the fact that it can save the lives of so many who suffer."

Sally was quiet for a while. "If that's what you want to do, I won't try to stop you."

"Look, Sally. I'm not that far away from you. Commack is only a few minutes away. I'll be available whenever you need me."

She put the phone down, looked at the half-eaten bagel and scrambled eggs still on her plate, and got up to make another cup of coffee.

She had barely finished her breakfast when the phone

rang. It was Martingale. He briefed her on the autopsy report and the likelihood of the nontrial.

Agnes was relieved. She dreaded a prolonged investigation and countless interviews with police and maybe with reporters, if there was to be a trial.

A pair of young pediatricians, fresh out of medical school, wanted to take over Owen's practice. They liked that Owen's office was located in a predominantly upper-middle-class neighborhood, and the likelihood of the established patients staying with the practice was great. The sale was completed without any hassle.

With the sale of Owen's practice out of the way, Agnes had one less thing to worry about. The proceeds from the sale were substantial. She was happy living by herself now that she had found a worthy cause in which to immerse herself. She was sure she could keep herself busy with her friends, and moreover, the impending grandparenthood filled her heart with joy.

"Life is what you make out of it, isn't it?" she whispered as she prepared to attend a meeting with the local NORML chapter.

Author's note: As of the writing of this book (December 2017), twenty-nine states have legalized the use of marijuana plants for medical purposes, and the number is expected to grow.

Ashok Shenolikar

ABOUT THE AUTHOR

Ashok Shenolikar lives in Fairfax, Virginia, with his wife Bharati. Ashok writes memoir, essays, short fiction and novels. His writing can be found at <u>ashokshenolikar.com</u>. He enjoys traveling around the world in his spare time.